GODCHILD

Kevin McNeil

DEDICATION

Godchild is dedicated to Micah's Promise.

ACKNOWLEDGMENTS

Thank you, loving and gracious Heavenly Father, for providing me with a gift to share with others. Without you, none of this would be possible.

To my mother, Lillie McNeil, thank you for loving me and for always believing in me.

To my editor and idea-partner, Nancy Karmiller, my deep gratitude for the steadfast and wholehearted energy you have given to this project; for the experience you brought and the conversations we had that helped bring these characters, and the book's message, to life.

To my eagle-eyed copy-editor, Jeannie Karmiller, for reviewing new drafts repeatedly; you have made this book infinitely clearer and more polished.

And lastly, I would like to thank my loving wife Tashanna, for her patience as I wrote this book, and even more for understanding and supporting my career path; God knew what I needed, and so He gave me you.

Micah's Promise is an organization in Columbus, Georgia that provides an environment for transformational life-change to survivors of Domestic Minor Sex Trafficking (DMST) by building a supportive community for reintegration.

Micah's Promise is committed to making a positive impact on DMST by raising the capital funds necessary to build a therapeutic treatment facility for girls aged 12 to 17 suffering from trauma associated with having been trafficked. Half the proceeds from the sale of this book are being donated to Micah's Promise to assist in this effort. For more information on Micah's Promise and how to support their mission, please visit: www.micahspromise.org

CHAPTER ONE

THE SOUND OF PEOPLE TALKING near her living room window woke Sarah from sleep. Lifting her head slightly, she scanned the room to ensure the voices were, indeed, coming from outside. The darkness made it difficult to see. Quietly, she placed one hand on the floor, feeling for her cell phone. Her racing heart and rapid breathing were the only things she could hear. The bare walls, empty shelves, and small living space functioned to make the two sounds louder. She remembered a TV commercial she had seen once, in which a yogi with flowing robes looked into the camera and said, *"Sometimes, you need to be in a place where the silence is deafening, for only there can you achieve inner peace."* She now wondered if she was experiencing the kind of silence the yogi was talking about. It certainly didn't feel like it.

Grabbing her phone, she hit the home button and quickly turned on the flashlight.

Nothing—her apartment was, indeed, empty.

Reassured, she allowed her body to plop back down onto the inflatable mattress. As she lay motionless, the smell of mildew and stale weed smoke assaulted her senses. It was obvious the apartment had not received a proper cleaning prior to her moving in, and as the morning light began to creep through the cheap plastic blinds and play across the walls, Sarah tried to picture the former occupants: passing blunts across the room with friends while laughing at stuff that wouldn't have seemed even remotely amusing to those not under its influence. She imagined the smokers, suffering from the ravenous hunger known as "the munchies," rummaging through the fridge and cussing when they found nothing. Almost immediately, she stopped imagining and looked around for any signs of bugs. She saw none and let out a huge sigh of relief. Sarah couldn't stand bugs. The thought of them made her skin crawl.

Gathering her thoughts, Sarah considered the time it would take for her to adjust to her new situation. Stifling a huge yawn, she sat upright and stretched her arms high above her head. It was time to wake up and prepare for her upcoming appointment. A glance at the digital clock showed it was only 6:40am.

Damn, don't these people have anything to do besides stand outside my window? she thought, as she heard the shuffling of feet outside. She hated the fact that her apartment was located in the rear of the complex, but the first-floor studio was all she could afford with her lean bank account. She hoped to own a more commodious home in the future, but had to be content with this one at the moment. She was still pissed though. When the apartment itself wasn't getting on Sarah's nerves, the constant foot traffic of the neighborhood kids going back and forth to the corner convenience store was beyond irritating.

The neighborhood was considered one of Atlanta's most dangerous, where the sounds of gunshots and people arguing outside at all hours made her uneasy. It was a far cry from Sarah's beginnings.

She had moved because she needed to, but damn, a part of her missed Buckhead, where the quiet walks and gated communities felt safe and gave her peace of mind. As her thoughts roamed on, she closed her eyes tightly, hoping to prevent the tears from flowing.

This was not the time to think about the past. It was time to get ready for the interview she hoped would lead to her first professional job— one she could be excited about.

The mattress made a squealing sound as she swung her slender legs over the edge. The sheets clung to her sweaty body as she sprang to her feet, her eyes focused momentarily on the painter's tape stuck to the air vent. The thermostat was not working and the movement—or lack thereof—of the painter's tape provided the only sign of heat or air conditioning. When she saw it was not moving, she muttered, "Dammit, they still haven't fixed the air." She pressed her lips together in an effort to keep the negative thoughts from multiplying. *Look on the bright side of things*, she thought. *Look on the brighter side.*

Entering the small bathroom, she heard more voices outside, which indicated that the city was stirring from its sleep. Picking up her toothbrush, she squeezed the tube's remaining toothpaste on it and turned on the water. The reflection she saw in the mirror made her cringe; she almost didn't recognize the image that stared blankly back at her. *It has been a while*, she thought as she ran her fingers down her cheeks. The lack of spa treatments made her look older, as her long, formerly straight hair was now kinky and in need of serious attention. It was as if she could hear the hair shouting "Mayday!" However, that was the least of her worries. A paycheck from her new job would take some time, and her funds, in addition to her beauty supplies, were running low. The small quantity of mouthwash left in the bottle was not enough to gargle with so she added a bit of water. She smiled weakly at her improvising. Even though she had a new bottle under the sink, she had to make it last. Money was tight and she wasn't about to waste anything.

As she ran the comb through her hair, she could still hear the sounds of people talking. Turning around abruptly, she grabbed the bathroom door and slammed it, half-yelling "shut the hell up already!" The brief moment of silence she earned was soon interrupted by more voices, which were no longer coming from the front of the apartment, but were now right under her bathroom window. Sarah turned the tap off so she could listen.

A deep baritone voice assaulted Sarah's ear: the speaker's anger came through very clearly as he warned his companion, "You better do what I tell you... this isn't a game!"

With the comb still in her hair, Sarah carefully pulled the cord that lifted the blinds and got up on her toes to better observe the events unfolding just outside her apartment. What she saw appeared straight out of a film scene: facing the building, no more than 10 feet away, a bald guy with a nicely trimmed beard, wearing an expensive-looking black Adidas jogging suit and looking like a pumped-up version of Samuel L. Jackson, was gripping a slight white woman by one skinny arm. As Sarah watched, the man yanked her close, appearing to whisper something in her ear—whatever it was made her cover her face and flinch. Then she jerked in a bid to get away from him and lost her balance, stumbling onto one knee on the pavement. As she braced herself against the asphalt with her hand to avoid falling totally flat, her long blond hair—evidently a wig—fell to the ground.

Sarah covered her mouth in disbelief and stepped back from the window. It was the first time she had witnessed a physical altercation in such an up-close and personal way, and though she wanted to stop watching, curiosity and concern got the better of her. Moving back to the window, she could see the woman, now lying curled up on the ground as the man stood over her. As Sarah watched, the woman rolled slightly away from him and rose awkwardly to her feet, snatching the wig from the ground and attempting to reposition it on her head as she half-ran in the direction of the street. That was when Sarah realized something else. The black leather skirt, fishnet stockings and red high heels had given the girl an older look.

"That's a child!" Sarah blurted, before quickly covering her mouth. Her sudden outburst echoed throughout the bathroom, and the man looked up, his narrow black eyes locking with hers before her trembling fingers could release the cord to close the blinds.

A glance at the clock reminded Sarah it was past time to get ready for her job interview. She could worry about the events outside her window later. Were she to land the job as a Court Appointed Special Advocate, she would be in a position to save many children, and it would mean the chance to leave the low wage jobs she'd held throughout college. Eventually, Sarah wanted to get her Master's in Counseling; that probably wouldn't be for a while, though, because after her parents stopped paying for school in her junior year, she'd had to increase her work hours, necessitating a reduced school schedule. This had extended the time it took to get her degree.

In addition, she had taken out student loans in amounts that now seemed even more insane than they had when Sarah—somewhat blinded by the desire to show that she didn't need her parents' approval of her chosen field, or their money—had eagerly signed the papers.

At this point the required payments were so high they'd kept her juggling multiple low-wage jobs, working 60-plus hours/week, since graduation. This interview might just be the ticket to something both more enjoyable and slightly more remunerative.

Removing her boxer shorts and tank top, Sarah jumped in the shower. She felt the warm streams of water flow down her smooth caramel skin, helping to relax some of the anxiety resulting from her morning's observations. Sarah turned off the shower and allowed her head to rest against the wall for a while, prolonging the few moments of peace. The relief was short-lived however, as her calm was shattered by recurring images of what she had just witnessed.

Getting out of the shower, she grabbed a towel and swiftly dried herself, then took a quick peep through the bathroom window where, to her relief, she saw no sign of anyone. Sarah tried to convince herself that the altercation was none of her business. Maybe the girl was a thief who had broken into a store and was caught by the angry storekeeper. Maybe she was a drug addict who hadn't paid for her high. The explanations Sarah created mentally didn't make sense but there was no way she was getting involved; she had a job interview to get to, and if she hurried, she could still make it on time.

As Sarah left her apartment and walked to her car, she was momentarily soothed by the chirping birds and the still-soft light of the morning sun.

———————

"Oh shit!" she whispered. The man she had seen from her bathroom window now stood in the parking lot, watching her as she walked quickly to the car on legs that suddenly felt like cooked spaghetti. She couldn't remember ever being so frightened. Nervously, her hand slid into her purse to feel for her can of pepper spray. "Shit," she muttered again as she remembered she had left it in the car. She grabbed her keys out of the purse, but her hands trembled and the keys fell to the ground.

Well, there goes playing it cool, she thought, as she picked up her keys and continued toward the car, hurriedly using her fob to unlock the driver's side door as she walked. Her breathing sounded as if she had just finished running a marathon.

When she reached the car, she grabbed at the door handle so fast her fingers slipped and she felt a searing pain as her nail bent backward. Her hands shook badly and she took a deep breath to calm herself while swinging the door open with her other hand.

As her butt plopped down in the driver's seat, she forced the key into the ignition and started the car. A quick glance in the side mirror showed the man leaning on a parked car near the entrance. She would have to drive right past him to exit the complex. *Maybe if I floor it and speed by, he won't get a good look at my face*, she thought. She immediately recognized it as a terrible idea, since the man already knew the apartment she lived in and the type of car she drove. His presence in the parking lot was clearly no coincidence. He had strategically placed himself right in front of a speed bump so Sarah would have to slow down as she passed him. She would have given anything at that moment to have tinted windows, but as the two front wheels crossed the speed bump, Sarah saw the man out of the corner of her eye lift his hand as if in a casual salute.

She knew it was no friendly gesture. It was clearly meant to remind her that he had seen her peering into his business. The evil eyes and hideous grin made Sarah's skin prickle—she had never felt so close to danger. She instinctively sped up at that moment, causing her two back tires to bounce so hard the rear bumper scraped the ground.

CHAPTER TWO

THE PLACE WAS CROWDED. WISPS of random conversations echoed throughout the establishment while soulful music from Kina Grannis played softly in the background. The patrons' soft chatter and sparkling jewelry reminded Sarah that she was in one of Atlanta's most prestigious country clubs; St. Ives. Located about twenty miles north of Atlanta's city limits in Johns Creek, Georgia, the community was home to some of the city's wealthiest residents. Sarah had grown up in this community before her family moved to Buckhead, about thirty minutes away, when she was six. She initially recognized no one as the stunning hostess led her through a maze of tables draped in white linen, each sporting a beautiful floral centerpiece and fine china. Soon, however, she spotted a familiar face, and turning to the hostess, she gestured in the direction of the bar,

"Okay, I see her, thank you."

As she approached the bar, the bartender gave her a warm smile, alerting her dinner date that she had arrived.

"Hi, Mother," Sarah said.

A beautiful African American woman dressed in a form-fitting purple dress turned from the bar and rose to her feet, her tall body instantly towering over Sarah's. Sarah wished, as she often did, that she had inherited some of her mother's height and strong features.

"Hi baby, thanks for coming. I have been so worried about you. Hey, Tom, you remember my baby, don't you?"

The bartender smiled, "Of course I do. What can I get you to drink, sweetie?"

Sarah replied, "Water with lime, no ice."

"Coming right up."

Placing both hands on Sarah's face, her mother examined her as though she were a hospital patient. "Baby, what happened to your hair? We have to get you in and let Louie do something with this mess. No daughter of mine can go around looking like someone from a homeless shelter." Sarah retreated a step while swatting her mother's hands away. "Mom! You sure know how to make a person feel missed."

"Sorry, sweetie. It's just...ever since you moved, your father and I have been worried sick about you..."

Sarah rolled her eyes.

"Here you go. It's great seeing you," the bartender said as he placed Sarah's lime-flavored water on a napkin in front of her. Sarah turned in her seat and smiled at Tom, but he had noted the look on her face as she and her mother began talking, and he respectfully stepped back to attend to other patrons.

"Okay, Okay, maybe not your father as much, but I've missed you. Why don't you come back home and give up this foolish dream of yours?" her mother asked, concern slowly creeping into her voice.

"You see Mother, this is why I don't like talking to you. You're always talking down to me. You and Dad don't understand I have my own life!"

"I know sweetie, but a social worker? What on God's green earth made you want to be a social worker?" her mother asked, while signaling for Tom to bring her another drink.

Sarah gave her mother a surprised look. She felt as if she was talking to another person, someone who had swallowed up her mother, like the wolf in the Little Red Riding Hood story. "I can't believe you! Rachel Clarkston, wife of Jacob Clarkston—did you forget the stories you told me of how you and Dad met?"

"Oh, now there you go, bringing up the past. That's your—"

Sarah cut her off, "Well, it didn't seem like a problem when you were telling me the stories. In fact, that's the only time I've ever really seen you happy—when you talked about how life was before you met Dad. You remember how you told me you two hated each other when you first met? You worked as a victim advocate and he was a public defender who defended their attackers and he kept calling you instead of the detective to get information. Then he finally came clean and asked you out on a date. Your face would light up as you recalled it. I looked forward to those times when you sat me on your lap and told me stories about helping people in need."

Looking at the lushly carpeted floor in deep thought, her mother responded, "Yes, your grandmother always taught us that *Love is God's currency that cannot be bought. Rather, you can only give and receive it.*" The two of them finished the quote in unison and then burst out laughing.

"I miss her so much, Mom."

"I know you do sweetie, so do I."

A little tear spilled down her mother's cheek and she dabbed it away with her fingers, "She would always tell me you were going to change the world. I just never wanted you to work in such a difficult, and terribly underpaid, field."

"But it's the work you loved. Okay, be honest Mom, why did you give up working as a victim advocate?"

"Girl, you know your dad. He insisted no wife of his would be working long, hard hours for low wages. Once he got his law degree, he expected me to quit working and make a home for him, and when you were born, he worked 80-hour weeks to give us the best of everything, leaving you and me alone. And while you were little, it was really an incredible gift to be able to spend so much time with you. I wouldn't have traded it for anything, even though I missed some aspects of my work. But after you started going to school, your father and I talked about it again, and he just said he thought it would take away from our family; that I would be too involved in the cases at work. I didn't like it, but I decided he was right." She sipped from the glass before her, and when the bartender made toward her to refill, she nodded a quick assent.

"Is that why you started drinking?"

Rachel's face froze momentarily as Sarah's question sunk in.

"Well, once you started going to school and you were participating in all those activities, you weren't home as much, and by the time you became a teenager, you didn't really need me—or at least you thought you didn't," Rachel said, with a wry look at Sarah. "And I got pretty lonely in that big house... I suppose alcohol became my companion."

Hearing this, Sarah wished she had not sounded judgmental, but she knew it had come out that way.

"See, Mom, you're unhappy because you gave up your passion. I will not allow that to happen to me. No amount of money in the world can take away my desire to become a social worker and I think it was totally unfair of Daddy to cut me off when I refused to change my major. He wants to use money to control me and I won't be manipulated."

Her mother slammed her drink on the bar, "Now look here young lady! Your dad busted his ass to provide a good life for us. You should show a little more gratitude for the life you were given. You know how many little black girls wish they had the things you've had? Your father's a hard-working man, and even if he's not always right, he only wants the best for you. Besides, despite what your grandmother says, it takes more than love to change the world; you are going to need money."

Sarah stood up. "Well, Mom, men aren't the only ones who have dreams. Women can dream too. Life isn't all about power, money, and success. I want to help people. What's so wrong with that?"

Before her mother could respond, a tall, handsome, light-skinned man walked up and placed his hand on her back, "Well if it isn't Rachel Clarkston! What brings you back to the old neighborhood?"

Her mother swung her head around, "Clifford!"

"How is my beautiful friend?" the man asked in a voice containing more than a hint of a smile.

"I'm fine. This is my daughter Sarah—you remember her, don't you?"

Sarah extended her hand and looked at her mom for an explanation. *Who was this handsome guy rubbing her mother and calling her by her name?* she wondered.

Her mother seemed to read her mind; "Darling, don't you remember Clifford? I guess it has been forever since you've seen him, but he was your father's roommate in college. They were like two peas in a pod. Your father the lawyer, Clifford the detective."

"Detective!" Sarah exclaimed.

"Yes, Ma'am, some people call me Detective Askew, and I think the last time I saw you, you called me 'Uncle Clifford.' But I haven't seen you in years—you must have been about five the last time I set eyes on you. It's wonderful to see you again, all grown up." He paused, "You look very much like your father—and I mean that as a compliment."

Before Sarah could respond, Clifford glanced at the Tag Heuer on his wrist, "Ladies, I must run, I'm meeting someone in the dining room, but it was truly a pleasure."

As he turned to leave, the detective flashed Rachel a smile. Sarah eyed his retreating figure and noted that his suit was perfectly tailored to his body. Although he was not young, his clean-shaven appearance made him look almost boyish.

Then, Sarah observed her mom's eyes watching Clifford as he walked away, and saw something was hidden beneath them. "Mom!" she gasped.

"What, girl, if your father and I hadn't gotten married, Clifford would have been a good dating match for me, although not a potential husband. He's definitely not as smart as your father, and I think he's one for the fast life, even now. But although Clifford flunked out of law school, he and your dad remained close friends for quite a while, though we haven't seen much of him these last years. Don't know how he does it but that man sure knows how to wear the finest suits."

Sarah turned around to see the detective speaking to a couple near the entrance. "So, does he work here?"

"No, sweetie, Clifford lives here. He has a beautiful ranch home overlooking a lake. It's located right near the sixteenth hole," Rachel said as she swallowed the last gulp of alcohol from her upended glass. "I don't know how he does it all on a detective's salary. But Clifford has always found a way to stay in the game with the major players. Jacob always said he was better suited to business than to law. He must have a business of some sort, I guess."

Sarah nodded, but her thoughts had moved on to dinner possibilities. Her eyes got big as she asked her mother, "Oh, do they still serve those delicious grilled prawns sautéed in that rich butter sauce?"

"They sure do. Hey Tom, we're ready to order!"

CHAPTER THREE

A TRICKLE OF SWEAT DRIPPED DOWN Sarah's nose as she placed her purse and cell phone on the conveyor belt. She looked in the direction of the female sheriff's deputy who motioned with her hand, "Right this way ma'am." Sarah stepped through the metal detector and gave the deputy a huge smile. She loved seeing women in predominantly male domains; it reflected the progress of the feminist movement, which she strongly supported.

Sarah's thoughts drifted back almost a decade, to a particular incident when she had confronted a staunch supporter of patriarchy, pointing out the flaws in his supposed logic. On that spring day when she was 16, she had been walking with a group of friends when they came upon a man protesting women's right to abortion; essentially the freedom to choose what happens to their bodies. While her friends had become emotional over the issue and hurled abuse at the guy, she had calmly walked up and asked to talk with him. He agreed, and when she asked him to help her understand why he was protesting, responded by expounding upon the need for the world to return to the time when women were confined to the role of caregiving within the home. He emphatically maintained that his mother had been, and still was, fully content with that role and this meant, to him, that all women should be satisfied with it. Even though a part of Sarah felt like punching the guy when he spoke, she restrained herself and instead began her line of questioning. She asked what his father did for a living. He answered that his father had been a plumber, and Sarah followed by inquiring if this was this man's job also. When he proudly told her that he was actually an artist at a tattoo shop, Sarah congratulated him on finding work that he found personally satisfying, and explained that in the same way, even though his mother might have loved the work of a caregiver, it did not mean that every woman would be happy in the same role.

Then, Sarah had asked the man if he had ever been raped. His immediate look of bewilderment and shock, tinged with just a bit of fear, was all the answer she needed to carry on with her pointed argument. She asked him to imagine being raped—and then, when it appeared he had at least spent a moment considering the level of violation that this would entail, told him that if he had ever been raped, he would understand the need for women to have the right to decide what happens to their bodies.

Finally, as she saw him nodding his head slightly at her statement, she told him that both men and women need to take responsibility for avoiding unintended pregnancies. Effective birth control has prevented more unintended pregnancies—and, consequently, abortions—than abstinence-only programs, which, like the "Just Say No to Drugs" programs of the 1980s and 90s, have been shown to be ineffective. Sarah had never seen anyone look as deflated as the former protester as he smiled wanly and turned to walk away.

Remembering the sense of accomplishment she had experienced when she had gotten through to this man, she smiled once more at the deputy, who waved a metal detector around Sarah's body and told her, "Okay, you're fine. Remove your items from the belt and have a nice day." Sarah grabbed her belongings and began looking for directions to the central office.

The vast lobby, with its soft music playing in the background and artwork on the walls, made her think she was in the wrong place. The space was immensely soothing and she compared the actual environment to how she had envisioned it. It was clear that the people who had designed it were cognizant of the science of environmental psychology. Families with children "in the system" have been traumatized in one way or another. Their states of mind tend toward the chaotic, and the last thing they need is to be surrounded by further sensory overload. On television and in the movies Sarah had watched, social services offices were always depicted as chaotic and noisy. She glanced at the address on the paper in her hand to make sure she was in the right location. It read, *Department of Family and Children's Services, 110 Sam Street, Decatur, Georgia 30032.* "Yes, this is the place," she murmured to herself as she admired the wonderful décor.

She located a directory in the middle of the lobby and pinpointed the central office directly to her right. It was hard to believe she was about to apply for a job that could set her firmly on the path toward her dream, and she began to feel little butterflies in her stomach. Sarah had been so happy when her mother agreed to ask Detective Askew to put in a good word for her; they both knew Jacob would be furious if he found out that Rachel was helping their daughter defy his wishes. It had not required much to convince her mother, however, because, as Sarah knew, her mother still loved efforts to improve the state of humankind. Sarah's mouth momentarily turned up in mirth as she considered the effects of upsetting her father. *Maybe he needed a taste of his own medicine,* she thought, as she imagined the shock on his face when he eventually found out about his wife's and friend's conspiratorial actions. However, she didn't want to tarnish the moment by thinking petty thoughts, so she banished them from her head. What she was about to do was important and she needed to be clear-headed in order to effectively articulate her qualifications to the person she hoped would eventually become her boss. Sarah quickly reviewed her appearance through her phone's camera to ensure she looked presentable. Then, she began to walk toward the office doors.

Once inside the waiting room, she saw a crowd of people and long lines. This was closer to what she'd been expecting from the DFCS office. While many people might see the mass of children and families packed in the small space and think twice about taking the job, Sarah Clarkston did not. She had been working toward this goal all her life. Her grandmother was a social worker and her passion had been reflected in Sarah's mother's similar devotion to social work until her marriage. *It's in my blood*, she thought, as she imagined having her own office and visiting families in need one day.

Sarah remained just inside the office doorway for a moment and took a deep breath. She was hopeful that Detective Askew's reference meant that she would be well received. After another short pause, Sarah inhaled deeply once again, shrugged her shoulders imperceptibly and checked in with the receptionist at the front, who handed her the paper application and a clipboard. She scanned the room for a place to sit and finally found one seat open among the teeming masses of people.

Sarah had just turned the application over to complete the second page when a little hand tapped her knee. Her eyes followed it and saw it was attached to the cutest kid she had ever seen. She was a little Latinx girl, not more than four years old, dressed in a pair of Batman pajamas, and her big brown eyes and silky black hair made Sarah want to pick her up.

"Hello there, what is your name?" Sarah chirped as her hand brushed the girl's hair.

The little girl turned her little hand over and made a begging gesture. Before Sarah could respond, the girl was snatched up by a visibly frustrated Latinx woman who had another small child strapped to her back.

"Lo siento, lo siento," the woman said, with an anxious expression. Despite Sarah's limited Spanish, she recognized the words as an apology for the child's interruption.

Sarah had been shaken by the abrupt manner in which the woman had grabbed the child, and she knew her face bore a look of concern, but it was clear that the woman had acted out of fear, so Sarah did what she could to reassure her, flashing a smile. She hoped that the woman would interpret her smile as a friendly gesture, and then looked down and continued to fill out the paperwork. She would already have finished if it had not been for her hesitation about the emergency contact page. Sarah shook her head as she thought about her current estrangement from her family—or her father at least.

She didn't want to put her father's name anywhere on the application, given the fact that she was going behind his back to get the job in the first place. Sometimes at her new apartment, Sarah would catch herself remembering the day she stormed out of her parents' house, bluntly shouting that she was done accepting his help. Now she carefully wrote her mother's name and cell number—not the home number—in the designated space.

The sound of a woman's voice broke her concentration. "Sarah—Sarah Clarkston!" she heard as she turned to identify the person speaking. On the other side of the room, Sarah saw a middle-aged African American woman scanning the crowd. Sarah identified herself by raising her hand, prompting the woman to gesture her over. Sarah wove her way through the maze of people. She extended her hand to shake that of the other woman; her interviewer, however, merely regarded her outstretched hand for a moment before inquiring tersely,

"Are you Sarah Clarkston?"

Obviously, handshakes are not part of the culture here, Sarah thought as she straightened up.

"Yes, I am."

"Okay, come have a seat in my office."

Sarah followed the woman to a small, cramped office dominated by clutter. The old office furniture and clunky, outdated desk computer surprised Sarah, as she thought an agency residing in such a beautiful building would be better equipped.

"I'm Barbara Cox, the office supervisor," the woman said by way of introduction, inviting Sarah to have a seat. "You can move those files out of the chair and make yourself comfortable."

Sarah reached down, grabbed the files and looked for a place to set the stack of bulging manila folders. As she attempted to place them in the adjacent chair facing the desk, she noticed it, too, was piled high and heard the woman mutter, "Place the damn things on the floor. As you can see, we're drowning in work."

Sarah turned to face her prospective boss and found her looking through the application she had just finished. Sarah waited for ten seconds and when she noticed that the woman was still preoccupied, she began to reflect on the fact that the place was not exactly what she would have expected of a supervisor's office. No fancy degrees on the wall. Also notably absent were the usual strategically-placed pictures of smiling family members. One photo, however, did catch her eye. It was of a younger-looking Barbara, someone who, while recognizable, appeared significantly different from the person sitting across the desk, frowning over Sarah's application. In the picture was a gorgeous, slim black woman in a tan two-piece bathing suit. Her curly hair wrapped around a beautiful round smiling face and the background appeared to be the bar or nightclub of some upscale tropical resort. Sarah contemplated asking her about the picture to introduce a bit of small talk about what looked as though it had been a happy time in the woman's life but her thoughts were interrupted when Barbara took a deep breath and asked, "What makes you want to be a Child Advocate?"

Sarah repositioned herself in the chair, "Well, I studied psychology and sociology in college and I have always wanted to—"

Barbara interrupted, "And don't give me any of that 'I want to save the children' bullshit. I have heard that before and those people don't last very long around here. They come in with high hopes and give up once the work gets to be too much. I'm tired of dreamers who see this shit on television and think it's a walk in the park. I was like that myself; now I know better. A few years in this system and you'll understand. Despite everybody's best intentions, nothing ever changes. The workload alone is crushing, and society isn't willing to put the resources into kids—they don't vote. You are the fourth applicant I've seen today, and I'm telling you up front that if you want to change the world, this isn't the place to do it."

Barbara's almost-hostile demeanor made

Sarah nervous, briefly putting her at a loss for words. What else could she say? The desire to help families was exactly her motivation for becoming a victim's advocate; however, Barbara Cox's words made her ask herself, *Are there any other reasons why I want this? What other reasons were there, though?* she wondered to herself. With an approximate starting salary of twenty-seven thousand dollars a year, she was certainly not in this office solely for the money. If that had been her primary consideration, she would have taken the job her father had offered her working in his firm. Sarah knew, though, that there was no way that she was going to let Barbara's bitter attitude dissuade her from her objective. It had taken an incredible amount of self-determination to get to the point of being able to apply for the job; the discouragement of this cynical civil servant was of no consequence given Sarah's resolve.

But how was she to make this clear when the last thing she'd expected to have to justify in this interview was her desire to help children!?

Sarah stuttered and tried, tentatively, to explain, "Well, well... I want to help children and families heal. Isn't that why you do it?"

Barbara snorted, leaned back in her chair and gave Sarah a sarcastic grin. "Humph, sure! Well, healing is not one of the things we do around here. We file stuff, take down information and report crimes to the police. As long as you can do that and be here on time, we might be able to use you."

Sarah's smile quickly dissipated as she saw Barbara put on her glasses, glance at her application, and remove them again. She knew that look and guessed that what came next would not be good.

"I'm looking at your application here and I remember that Detective Askew recommended you. How do you know him?"

The question made Sarah uneasy. Although she didn't want her father's help, she knew his name might give her a better chance at getting the job—something that was of vital importance, given her lack of relevant job experience. She shifted in discomfort and gulped before answering.

"Um, he and my father went to college together."

"Your dad..." Barbara paused and her eyes narrowed,

"Is Jacob Clarkston your father?" she queried in apparent surprise, as she glanced back down at Sarah's application. "And yet I see you've been working for Aldi as a grocery clerk since 2015. Humor me here; you mean to tell me your father doesn't have any fancy jobs waiting for you down at the law firm?" Barbara's snide tone was unmistakable. It seemed she enjoyed this digression from the formal interview questions introduced by her discovery of Sarah's father's identity.

"Well, I've always wanted to be in social work like my mother. I thought maybe—" Sarah sensed rejection—and perhaps even a lecture—coming and her shoulders slumped in defeat. So many people had felt the need to tell her how to live her life. She was used to being questioned about this choice, whether by her father, mother, their friends, other relatives, etc.—this was the reason she had insisted on becoming independent in the first place. Now, she was beginning to regret applying for the job with the recommendation of her parents' friend. *If she had just applied by herself with no connection to her family. If only—* Sarah started to respond but Barbara cut her off.

"I tell you what. Because Detective Askew recommended you, I will give you a chance, even though you don't have any previous, relevant experience—except babysitting, and I will tell you right now, this is *nothing* like babysitting. But I guess you'll see for yourself," she added, clearly done with the interview.

Sarah didn't like the harsh comments, but given that she had steeled herself for rejection, she was, if not elated, extremely pleased. She had just been given the opportunity she craved. She stood up and extended her hand to Barbara.

Barbara looked up from her desk and stared at Sarah. "Thank me later."

Sarah bent over to replace the files in the seat, but Barbara snapped, "Leave them and close my door behind you!"

As the door closed, Barbara picked up her cell phone and dialed Detective Askew.

CHAPTER FOUR

THE SMELL OF FRESH COFFEE filled the room as Sarah sat at the kitchen table reading. She loved the smell, and she had discovered that the combination of coffee and reading seemed to have an unexpectedly calming effect on her, no matter what she was reading. The book she had chosen this particular morning was *Without Consent*, a powerfully evocative murder mystery by former FBI profiler Jim Clemente. It had been three days since she started the book, so she should have been well into the gripping parts, but as her eyes followed the pages, her mind wandered to all the cases awaiting her at the office.

It was Monday, the day of the week that Barbara seemed to love most. It was the day on which she gave out new cases to the workers, each of whom would groan as the new assignments added to the pressure of their already onerous caseloads. The distress of those under her never seemed to matter to Barbara, and Sarah expected that today would be no exception.

I wonder what kind of demanding case will Barbara send me now? Sarah wondered, as she thought of her office voicemail. She knew it would be full of messages from anxious parents calling about the status of their cases; single mothers asking if their kids could be returned to them and fathers concerned about the particulars of a case. Sarah knew that while society still adhered to a fairly traditional model when it came to dividing up child-care duties, men were starting to become more involved in daily parenting, which meant that they were often equally affected by the removal of a child.

One of her cases involved Tara, a single mother who was having problems raising her kid properly. When she was 21, she had given birth to a baby whose father went on to be incarcerated before the child turned two. Although Tara had wanted to stay connected with her baby's dad, the exorbitant cost of phone calls from prison had made that nearly impossible, and the difficulty of life as a single parent without reliable daycare—the state would pay for daycare, but the rate they allowed was so low that only a few in-home centers would accept it, and they were all full—had led to Tara's losing her job. Life had gone from bad to worse when Tara developed depression, leading to the terrible living environment that had prompted Tara's neighbors to call child protective services. Although attempts had been made to connect Tara with the medical and mental health services she needed, lack of transportation, money and social support exacerbated her situation, contributing to her inability to get back on her feet. The child had been in the system for about five months now, with Sarah having taken on the case when she started three months ago, but despite Sarah's best efforts to get Tara the help she needed, something was always getting in the way.

The foster parents were going above and beyond what was required of them, supervising frequent visits with the mother, and even ferrying the child to and from the prison one weekend per month because they knew that the chances of the father remaining engaged in his child's life, and his chances of staying out after he was released, were far greater if he could maintain this bond during his incarceration. Still, the enormity of the myriad obstacles facing this family were beginning to dawn on Sarah, and she had to admit that she was beginning to question her own role in this system.

Sarah had never imagined that making a difference would be so difficult. She was beginning to consider that Barbara might not have been overstating the case when she said that the work would break Sarah's zeal for healing the world. Sarah was determined that this would not happen to her, but the sheer volume of the workload—coupled with the sense of powerlessness to effect real change—was definitely challenging. She hoped that things only felt so overwhelming because she was still relatively new to the job, and that once she had learned all of the ins and outs of the paperwork, court system procedures, and resources she would have more time to spend on the part that mattered—the kids—but she was beginning to have doubts.

Sarah lifted her mug and drained the last swallow of coffee. After placing the mug in the sink, she walked into her bathroom to finish getting ready. She had gotten used to the apartment by now and the sounds didn't generally bother her much. However, she looked into the mirror and shook her head sadly as she noticed that her blouse had a small but distinct stain over her left breast—a remnant, perhaps, of the spaghetti lunch she'd brought to the office last week—there was always *something*!

"Ugh," she uttered as she adjusted her jacket. She hoped no one at the office would notice. She looked into the mirror once again, prepared to admire her physique. But she was getting thin. Before she started her new job, she wasn't by any means fat; however, the figure reflected back at her in the mirror seemed to have lost more than 10 pounds. She figured that the number might be exaggerated, but there was no disputing the fact that she was significantly skinnier than before.

"I need a break," her mind started to say, before immediately recognizing that she was working more than ten hours a day just to try to stay on top of things; she couldn't imagine what it would be like if she actually left, even just for a long weekend.

In fact, there wasn't even time to change her clothes as it was already late and she didn't want to get caught in the morning traffic.

Sarah heard voices as she exited her apartment and walked toward the stairs. She wished there was another way to get to her car. Every morning brought the distasteful harassment of the men who loitered outside her building. Such men seemed to be present in many apartment blocks around the city. She would see them share bottles of Jack Daniels while they tossed lewd "compliments" at women who passed. Sarah often pretended to be on the phone when she encountered the men, but she did not even bother this morning.

"Hey there business lady, why don't you ever speak?" a middle-aged black man called teasingly as Sarah reached the bottom of her stairs. He was now so close that she could smell a bit of alcohol coming from his breath as she gave him a quick glance and flashed a frown. The fool who had decided to bother her that morning was just Scooter, her downstairs neighbor. He was in his fifties and lived with his mother, who allowed him to stay because his mental illness entitled him to monthly disability checks. Sarah sometimes pitied the man because he seemed harmless, and as though he had given up on life because of his disability. This had driven him into the embrace of the bottle and it was rare to see him sober. He wasn't a bad guy, though, as far as Sarah could tell, and the kids in the neighborhood loved hanging out with him because he gave them spare change whenever he could.

As Sarah opened her car door and slid into her car seat, she heard Scooter yell again, "Hey, why you don't speak?" Getting angrier, she quickly slammed her car door shut and drove away—she did not wish to scream a loud "fuck you!" to anyone on a Monday morning.

As she drove onto the road, her phone began to ring. When she checked the screen, she saw that it was Barbara and her heart skipped a beat. Before she answered, she glanced at the clock on her dashboard and noted that it was only ten minutes past eight. That meant she wasn't late.

As she mulled over the call, she was tempted to allow it to go to voicemail. However, she decided against it as avoiding her boss was likely to create more trouble for her later.

"Hello. Good Morning." Sarah feigned a composure she did not feel as she picked up the call.

The voice on the other end was curt and direct, "I need you to go to the Juvenile Detention Center and speak with a juvenile. We need to find her a placement until her court date. She doesn't have enough points for a juvenile hold."

Sarah heaved a sigh of relief, then replied.

"I'm driving now. Can you text me the information?"

She could sense Barbara's inexplicable offence at the request.

"There is nothing to text, her name is Aviela Scott." With that, Barbara hung up the phone.

"Damn you Barbara," Sarah said as she began to mentally recalibrate the route that she was going to take to reach the juvenile center.

Aviela Scott, Aviela Scott, she murmured, so that she would not forget the name before she reached the location.

Even though Sarah had not gone alone to the juvenile center before, she had accompanied another worker and noted the route. Diana, the social worker who took her, made sure that Sarah knew the fastest way to get there from the office, but now, driving from her home, Sarah knew she would need to use the mapping function on her phone. Trying not to take her eyes off the road, Sarah asked Siri to find the Juvenile Justice Center. Soon she could see the familiar structure of the facility taking shape ahead, and she smiled with relief. She quickly ran through a mental checklist of the questions she knew she would need answers to, and parked in the near-est parking spot.

"Hello. I'm here to see Aviela Scott," Sarah stated, as she flashed her ID at the security officer.

"Wait right there," the officer responded, as he pointed to a table with two chairs facing each other. Sarah looked around the drab waiting room. When she heard the door open, she turned to meet the girl, but when the teenager entered the waiting room, Sarah could barely believe her eyes.

The girl being led toward her was the same person she had seen being assaulted behind her apartment building. Although it had been months, Sarah recognized the girl's face immedi-ately, but she looked different from the way she had on that early morning–very different.

So this is why the detention center didn't want to house her. Aviela Scott was pregnant.

The girl in her blue jumpsuit stood only about five feet tall. Her brown hair was braided in corn-rows, which did not match her freckled face. She sat down opposite Sarah, not recognizing her at all. Sarah noticed that although her stomach was protruding from her clothing, Aviela's thin arms and legs, and the narrow face that looked up at her, still belonged to a little girl, and it was shocking to imagine her having to care for a baby, as she soon would.

"Hello. My name is Sarah Clarkston. I have been assigned to your case and I have a few questions for you if you like." At that moment, Sarah realized how silly she sounded. Of course the girl would not like to answer any questions. She certainly would not like staying at the juvenile facility, cut off from her freedom, and living under the myriad rules that ostensibly served to keep the youth safe, but in fact often had more to do with imposing a sense of the overpowering authority of the system, as it often allowed and forbade things without any apparent rational.

The young girl leaned back in her chair and crossed her arms, a sign of hostility that neither surprised nor fazed Sarah.

"Okay, I will take that as a 'Yes.' Let's start with your name."

The girl snapped, "It's Aviela Scott, but you knew that already."

Sarah looked up from writing and across the table. She felt a small smile tug at the corner of her mouth, as she looked at the girl with kind eyes. She knew that the girl's defenses were there for a reason, and she relished the challenge inherent in helping her build trust that Sarah was on her side.

"I like your hair. I wish my hair was thick enough to get cornrows," Sarah said, smiling.

The compliment seemed to have little effect; though Aviela unfolded her arms and sat up straight, her frown was still firmly in place. "Who did you say you are again?"

"Sarah Clarkston. I'm from the Court Appointed Special Advocates' Office."

"You not a cop?"

"No. I'm not. I'm here to get you out of this place," Sarah answered, hoping it would mollify Aviela.

"Well, I'm not going back to that damn hell hole you call a youth program," Aviela suddenly said, relaxing back in her chair and folding her arms again.

What an attitude you got on you, little missy, Sarah thought, both amused and saddened that the girl had been required to develop such a hard shell to survive. Gently, she responded,

"Okay, I hear that. You want to tell me why?"

Her eyes locked defiantly on Sarah's, Aviela slowly shook her head.

Sarah looked back at the paper in front of her. "It says here that you have a court date tomorrow. Where do you want the judge to send you?"

"I really don't care as long as it's not there."

Sarah looked at her and made the decision, based upon girl's implacable stare, that it would be futile to send her back to her old youth program. "Then I will see what I can do."

"Really?" Aviela responded in apparent surprise.

"Yep. Prepare your stuff"

Grabbing her things, Sarah rose and extended her hand toward Aviela.

Aviela looked at the outstretched hand, as if unsure of how to respond. She then balled up her fist, extended her arm and gave Sarah an awkward fist-bump.

"Thank you," Aviela said as she allowed herself to be escorted back to her cell.

CHAPTER FIVE

I T WAS A BEAUTIFUL DAY in the city. Visitors, commuters and employees crowded the narrow streets of downtown Atlanta. Every few blocks a panhandler interrupted a passing pedestrian to ask for money. The lunch crowd was thinning, and as she drove back toward the office, Sarah saw a parking spot open up right in front of a shop she'd been wanting to check out. Cars blew their horns as Sarah stopped her car abruptly in the middle of the road and began backing into the small parking space. *They are too impatient,* she thought as she focused on maneuvering the vehicle. She sometimes wondered why folks were in such a damned rush. Hearing the loud growl of a revving engine, she glanced left in time to see a small red Mini Cooper speeding past; it nearly took off her front bumper.

She exited the car and placed quarters in the parking meter, quickly checking the time on the white-faced Movado her parents had given her for her twentieth birthday. She wore it not so much as a timepiece—her phone could have told her that—or even a fashion statement, but to remind herself of those better days. She walked briskly toward the quirky resale shop that had piqued her curiosity, despite its limited external appeal. Even though she didn't plan to stay long, she knew that when it came to window shopping, she tended to lose track of time. Her lunch break was ending in fifteen minutes, but her interest in the shop trumped her sense of urgency to return to work. The painted letters on the window, spelling out *Kyle's*, looked as though they had been drawn by a first-grader hustling for money to buy video games. The letters were constructed of big cursive loops and each was a different color. If the sign was created to draw attention, it worked. As Sarah drove by on her way to and from work each day, she saw people streaming into and out of the small store, nestled as it was between a barber shop and a Vietnamese restaurant.

The scents from lit candles delighted Sarah as she stood in the doorway, and as she glanced around, her eyes took in one of her favorite Maya Angelou quotations hanging on the wall. It reminded visitors, "People may not remember what you say, or what you do, but they will always remember how you made them feel." Sarah appreciated the sentiment; it was one to which she could personally attest. Her mind flashed back to an incident that had occurred five years previously when she had witnessed a mugging. She had been walking down the street with a friend when an elderly woman just a few feet away had had her bag jacked by a young man sporting a red hoodie.

While Sarah's friend had immediately rushed to sucker-punch the thief, Sarah had tended to the victim. When it was all over, the woman told Sarah that while she was certainly grateful the thief had been apprehended and she hadn't lost her purse, Sarah's warm and comforting presence had been equally important to her emotional wellbeing during the experience.

Sarah made her way to the back of the store where a sign identifying the sale items hung. Before she could reach the rack, a mannequin wearing a beautiful midnight blue dress caught her attention. As she moved toward it, she couldn't believe her eyes. Instantly, she felt a breath of her former life wash over her; her mother favored the designer Alexander McQueen, and, if she wasn't mistaken, had once had this very dress, albeit in a different color.

Sarah was a little shocked to see an Alexander McQueen sitting in a resale shop and she surveyed it, wrapped perfectly, as it was, around the mannequin. Sarah momentarily envisioned herself attired in the dress, being twirled to the sounds of Strauss in a perfect Viennese waltz on the floor of an imaginary ballroom. The scenario included the admiring looks and enthusiastic applause of her fantasy audience. Sarah mentally shook herself free of the image. Her hands carefully searched for the price tag. "Hmmm... just three hundred and forty-nine dollars!" In reality, it didn't matter because she didn't have this kind of money to spend on a dress, but it didn't mean that she couldn't appreciate its beauty. Also, the connection to her mother made Sarah feel oddly, unexpectedly, at home here. Quickly, she turned her attention to the adjacent rack full of various high-end brand blue jeans. As she felt the texture of the clothes, she thought of all the money she could have saved shopping at Kyle's rather than Phipps Plaza. She chuckled to herself and reached for a pair of jeans that looked just her size, finding on the rack next to them several dresses that looked intriguing.

A male voice came from over her shoulder. "Well, I see someone has good taste."

Sarah turned to see a slender man about her height, with jet-black glossy hair in the latest fashion with the sides cut short and the top caught back in a short ponytail that adorned the top of his head. He was dressed in skinny black jeans and a black T-shirt which read "Only God can judge me," a motto Sarah identified with people who did not give a flying fuck about others' opinions. The man wore a pair of red suspenders over thick shoulders that reminded her of those of a swimmer.

As Sarah took a closer look at his face, she realized that she was looking at a natural-born model. He had sapphire-blue eyes, which, contrasting with his deep umber skin, were as enthralling as anything Sarah could have imagined. She couldn't identify his ethnic background, but she was quite sure that he must have every girl within a mile under the spell of his stunning good looks. His mien was calm and collected, but he radiated such warmth and intensity that Sarah found herself wondering if he was this electrifying with everyone, or if he was singling her out for special attention. Either way, it was no wonder that the place always seemed abuzz with people.

The man flashed a half smile and extended his hand, "Hello, I've never seen you in the store before. Would you like to try something on?"

He had a perfect set of milky white teeth, and Sarah felt his charm working on her. He had on ordinary white high-top canvas sneakers which only served to highlight his other, rather unique, sartorial selections. Sarah loved innovative fashion choices because they were generally worn by rebels who created their own paths, which they traversed with heads held high.

"Maybe," she responded, "I'm kinda in a hurry, but you do have some very nice things in here. I must admit, I was pleasantly surprised. Judging from the outside of the store, I wasn't sure what to expect." Sarah smiled warmly to show she meant no disrespect. She heard the door of the shop open as another customer walked in and hoped the handsome salesman would not leave her in order to attend to the other shopper. He smelled good. Sarah paused long enough to inhale deeply—it confirmed her suspicions—he was wearing Tom Ford's *Black Orchid* and it was absolutely amazing on him.

"Well, we can't always judge things by the way they look on the outside, now, can we?" he asked rhetorically, tilting his head and inspecting the clothes Sarah had pulled from the racks and which were now draped over her right arm. He moved in even closer, and then, without asking permission or even seeming aware of their extreme proximity, began rifling through them, murmuring "yes, maybe this one" and "no, that's not for you" as he took them from her one by one. He then turned back to the rack of dresses she had just consulted. As Sarah watched, she noticed that he seemed to favor flowery dresses over plain ones and she began to feel a little annoyance at his presumptuousness. Soon, however, he had a dress that looked great in his hands and he thrust it at her, saying with blithe confidence, "This will look fabulous on you— don't bother about any of the other things. This is the only one you need."

Stepping back with a look, Sarah blurted out, "Oh really?" and then, not even sure whether she was more amused or irked, she continued,

"Excuse me, but does the owner know how you treat customers?"

The man winked and pointed to the rainbow-colored sign above the cash register that read "Kyle's."

"I'm Kyle."

"Ahh," said Sarah, laughing in spite of herself. "That's how you get away with it! Well, hello Kyle, my name is Sarah, and it's nice to make your acquaintance." With the realization that Kyle's confidence must be a key element of his shop's success, Sarah found herself enjoying their banter, and thinking about how little social interaction she had outside of her work these days. She took the dress he proffered and held it up, imagining herself in it. A green dress with a flower design, it looked like the kind of dress that one could wear on a date. Looking at it again, she imagined that it would be the perfect kind of dress to put on when going to meet her boyfriend's parents, if she ever acquired a boyfriend, that is. She smiled and said, "You're right, Kyle. This seems as though it would fit me perfectly. And what would you recommend for a work outfit?" Sarah grinned playfully as she raised one eyebrow and surveyed his own outlandish outfit, making it clear she was teasing him.

Kyle laughed a bit loudly and quickly covered his mouth while looking to see if other customers were watching. Seeing that everyone was engrossed in their shopping, he motioned for Sarah to follow him. He led her to a mannequin wearing a tank top over distressed jeans, exclaiming, "Taa daaa! If you want to follow my lead, here is the perfect outfit to almost definitely get you fired from your office."

"Yeah, there is absolutely no way you will get me in that on a weekday," Sarah said as she laughed. She noted that for the first time in a while, she was with someone who made her laugh. "Okay then, Kyle, I will give it some thought, and I might just return to get that top. Deal?"

"Deal," he replied.

Sarah paid for the dress, which she noticed he had discounted an extra twenty percent, and carefully put her credit card back in her purse.

Kyle reached over the counter, grabbed a business card and paused for a moment before saying, unexpectedly, as he handed it over; "I really would like to see you again. I'm not coming on to you—I'm gay—but I like your energy, and I hope to see you back here sometime soon."

Sarah smiled, slightly surprised at Kyle's straightforwardness, but aware she felt the same way. Reaching down to take the card, she saw what appeared to be the faded scars of multiple parallel scratch marks on his satiny, caramel-colored skin. Instinctively, Sarah wanted to ask him if they were the result of his cutting himself. However, remembering that he was still a stranger, and therefore reasonably likely to take offence at the sudden intrusion into his private life, she kept silent and pretended not to notice, but as she walked away, Sarah knew that she would definitely be back to see him before too long.

CHAPTER SIX

THE TENSION BETWEEN THE TWO men was as sharp as a chef's blade, and similarly piercing. Side by side they faced the silver doors as the elevator rose, silently eyeing each other's reflections.

BING!

The loud chime signaled that they had arrived at their destination. As they stepped off the elevator onto the twenty third floor, they were immediately greeted by Abraham, the ever-helpful custodian Jacob had hired a couple of years back when the company that had initially handled the maintenance went belly up. Abraham now moved quickly to open one of the large glass doors leading to the reception area. "Good afternoon, gentlemen," Abraham greeted them, holding the door while standing courteously off to the side; Clifford swept through without a sign that he had heard the man, but Jacob dipped his head in recognition as they passed.

As the door shut behind the men, they continued on toward the receptionist's desk, their brisk strides speaking of determination and purpose. Their movements caused staff members to part on either side of them. Clifford's eyes drank in the details of the décor, including the impressive sign behind the receptionist's desk, where a bright gold set of letters combined to form "Clarkston Law Firm." It covered the back wall behind a large U-shaped mahogany desk.

Looking at the face behind the receptionist's desk, Clifford flashed a broad smile at the beautiful, middle-aged white woman who smiled briefly in return, with a quick glance at Jacob, as if to ask who this cheery-looking man might be. When it became immediately clear that Jacob was not in such a smiley mood, her focus instantly returned to her computer screen and she began pecking away again at the wireless keyboard.

On each side of the receptionist's expansive desk stood magnificent bouquets of fresh flowers, artfully arranged in the current fashion that bordered on slight disarray, as though they had just been plucked from a field and placed, with the attendant leaves and ornamental grasses, into enormous cut glass vases.

A waterfall flowed from the front of the desk into a small, enclosed aquarium located at the base. Several fish, seemingly representing all the colors of the rainbow, swam at the bottom of the aquarium, oblivious to the events of the world above them. The desk appeared to be floating, giving those speaking with the receptionist the illusion that they were walking on water.

"Well, well, I must say, this is impressive!" Clifford uttered as he looked toward his companion, sensing from Jacob's lack of response that he was uninterested in Clifford's reaction to his surroundings. "Of course," Clifford followed, "the new virtual-reality games the kids are all talking about are able to create this kind of feeling, and for a lot less money."

Jacob spoke calmly and naturally, "Hey, let's get this over with, I got work to do." He frowned at the receptionist and in a brisk tone said, "Hold my calls, Mary."

Tensing, the blond-haired receptionist looked up at him. "Sure, Mr. Clarkston."

When Jacob Clarkston spoke, everyone in the building attended to his wishes as quickly and unobtrusively as possible. The handsome, charismatic man was one of Decatur, Georgia's most successful lawyers. The muscles on his 6'3" frame suggested a commitment to working out, and he was not above using his size to manipulate jurors, above whom he towered intimidatingly. There were whispers in the legal community that even some judges were intimidated by his physique and demeanor. The office reflected his position of power in the city, the only African

American business owner to occupy the top floor of the Bank of America building.

The climb to the top hadn't been easy for him. Jacob had grown up off Glenwood Road, an impoverished area of Atlanta often referred to simply as "the ghetto." Like so many of his peers, he had found himself in perpetual legal trouble and had nearly ruined his life before it had fully begun. He attended school irregularly and enjoyed wandering the streets, shooting dice with friends and fighting with rival gangs. The Atlanta Journal had done a story tracing Jacob's path from juvenile delinquent to successful attorney. When he got a copy of the issue, he had held it close to his heart.

Now, in the building where he was boss, he was meeting with the man who had helped him get here, his college best friend Clifford Askew. He was the man the Atlanta Journal had failed to acknowledge, but Clifford knew the reason he was not part of that story.

The two men walked through another set of doors that led to a narrow hallway. In offices on either side of the hallway were accountants, paralegals, and lawyers busy working on cases. Jacob led the way as Clifford followed, stretching his head into each office, waving and saying hello to employees who were bent over papers, coffee machines, and photocopiers. It was as if Clifford was hoping that Jacob would stop and introduce him. That wish was never granted, however, and they continued on until they made a sharp left when they got to the end of the hall and walked about twenty feet.

The sight of two large wooden doors with dark tinted windows on each side told Clifford they had arrived at Jacob's corner office. Jacob flashed the key fob in front of the little gray box on the left side of the doors and stood aside so Clifford could enter, giving him a cold stare as he did so.

The two men entered the office and once again, Clifford stopped, took a quick look around and smirked as he read the words in a blue frame that hung on the right wall of the office close to Jacob's desk. He hummed the words as he saw Jacob shake his head, *"Micah 6:8 'He has shown you, O' mortal, what is good. And what does the Lord require of you? To act justly and love mercy and to walk humbly with your God."*

Jacob irritably interrupted Clifford's humming, declaring "Man, you know that was my mom's favorite scripture? They were the last words she spoke to me before losing her battle with pancreatic cancer."

"Remember when I first brought you to my house and she asked you your favorite Bible story? All you could say was the story of Moses. You didn't know a damn thing about Moses," Jacob continued. Clifford chuckled, but realized almost immediately that Jacob had not intended this reminiscence as a bonding moment. Belatedly, Clifford recognized that Jacob was not amused.

Now Clifford walked over to the corner of the office and stood in front of the thick glass that stretched from the floor to the ceiling. Placing his hands on his hips he said reflectively, "You know, after fighting crime for nearly twenty years, a person can almost forget how beautiful ordinary life can be."

There was still rock-solid silence from Jacob, who now seemed to be preoccupied with other thoughts. Clifford glanced over his right shoulder to see if his friend was still listening and noticed that Jacob was hunched over his phone, responding to a text message on his cell phone. "What's wrong, buddy? You too busy for an old friend?" Clifford said with a provocative smile meant to infuriate Jacob.

The smile did the trick as Jacob squinted in annoyance at Clifford and placed his cell phone on the desk. Slowly, he removed his suit jacket, sat down in his chair and powered up his computer. His silence reminded Clifford that he was in no mood for small talk.

Clifford looked through the glass windows once again, "Nice view you got here. Looking out this window sure reminds me of the promised land. So, this is what it must have felt like for Moses being on top of the mountain. I've got to give it to you Jacob; you know how to play the game."

"Cut the bullshit Clifford, what do you want?"

"Now, now, is that any way to treat an old friend? Especially one who helped you get into this nice office?" Clifford snapped back. He would not be cowed by anyone, not even by Jacob and his intimidating frame.

"As I told you before Clifford, there will be no more payments. I'm going legit now, and while it's not as though I don't appreciate everything you've done for me, the stakes are greater now and I've got much more to lose."

Clifford saw that as an opening, promptly retorting, "You should have thought of that when I was tampering with state's evidence and risking my career to make you look good."

"Oh, don't act like you weren't benefiting from it, too. I paid your ass two thousand dollars a case!" Jacob said, his voice rising.

"And I made your ass the most successful defense attorney in Atlanta! You know how many criminals you put back on the streets?"

"You mean WE, we put back on the streets," Jacob corrected him.

Both men realized they were raising their voices and became briefly silent. They had come up in the ghetto, where the streets were always listening, and they both knew the importance of speaking softly. Jacob rose and walked toward his friend who stood waiting for a response. Jacob took two more steps before stretching his right hand forward as a signal for a truce. "Hey

Cliff, just let things be. We both got paid and no one got hurt. Why can't you let it go? No one told you to live such an expensive lifestyle, you should have put the money to better use."

Seeing that Jacob wasn't going to break, Clifford spurned the handshake with a gentle slapping away. "Naa braah. It doesn't work that way."

The two men stood side by side staring out the window. It was the first time they had fallen out since college, and now they could feel that their friendship and livelihood both stood on the edge of an abyss. Clifford checked his watch and paused briefly before raising the stakes; "You know, Jacob, I'm not the one with a young daughter now living in Atlanta's roughest neighborhood. I'm sure one of the thugs you let out of jail would be glad to get hold of her."

"You keep my fucking family out of this, Clifford! I'm warning you!" Jacob snarled as he bared his teeth in anger.

"Jacob; don't be stupid. All I'm saying, man, is that I can still be your inside guy in the department; give you information, do background checks, run tags, and give you access to detective notes." Clifford slapped Jacob on the shoulder, "Come on, we will be partners again. What would that wife and pretty little daughter of yours think about their successful hero if they knew his dirty secret?" He paused before continuing, "You know I saw the two of them at the old country club last week."

Surprise was written all over Jacob's face, "What the hell are you talking about Clifford?"

"See, that's just what I mean. I can be your eyes and ears again man. Hell, you can't even keep up with what your wife and daughter are up to. How are you going to get all the leads you need for your high-profile cases now? And you're damn right, the stakes are higher. You won all those cases as a defense attorney because of the information I provided you. You remember how I botched some of my cases to make you look good? Do I need to remind you of some of the other things I did? How about that time I removed property from the evidence locker, or the time I forgot to do a chain of custody. Need I continue? I know you remember. What is going to happen when you start losing cases all of a sudden?"

Jacob sat in his seat and pretended not to be bothered. He wondered why Rachel had not mentioned that she had spoken with Clifford. "I'm sorry, but I can't afford to do this any longer. Besides, if you tell the truth, you will lose your precious job as well."

Standing fully erect, Clifford stared Jacob down, "Well, friend, as you said, you have more to lose than I do. So try me"

"Get the hell out of my office bef..."

"Before what, before you call the police? Clifford extended his phone to Jacob "Go ahead, call."

When he saw that Jacob hesitated, he placed his phone back in his pocket, "That's what I thought, Jacob. Tell you what, I will make a deal with you. Hand over your little black book with your clients' information, and I will disappear from your life. Then I won't have to tell those two sweet ladies of yours how old Jacob 'The Trickster' Clarkston really made it to the top of the mountain. And don't tell me you don't have it because I know how you operate."

Jacob froze, knowing in that moment that this was why Clifford had engineered the meeting here today. Jacob had always had an almost obsessive need to keep notes on the various cases he and Clifford had rigged. He was careful to use a kind of simple code, and he knew better than to keep the information on the computer where it would be accessible to any hacker, but he should have considered that the greatest danger might come, not from an outside investigation in which his computer might be seized, but from his once close friend, and "partner in crime," Clifford.

Jacob knew there was no point in denying the existence of the log, but he was struggling to wrap his brain around the fact that Clifford was essentially giving him no choice. Almost numb with shock, he said, "Those guys would kill me if they knew I gave their information to the police.

Are you trying to place my family in jeopardy? I knew you were desperate for power and money, but I didn't know you would be willing to destroy my life for it."

Clifford's smile widened as he extended his hands one more time. He seemed to be enjoying the moment. "What exactly did you think? That I would simply go away once you decided you didn't need me anymore? No, man, you got yours, and I'm still getting mine. Just hand over the book and I will go away—I'll have another source for the funds I need, and you can settle into this life of luxury you built on my back."

Jacob plopped back into his seat. His shoulders slumped in defeat, he looked up and his eyes became glued to a picture of his family. The silver frame had the words *Family First* engraved at the top and was taken during a family trip to Disney when Sarah was just eight years old. He grabbed it and placed it face down on his desk. Glancing at his computer's screensaver, a picture of a smiling Sarah standing with Minnie Mouse at Disneyworld, almost brought a tear to his eye. Her toothless smile, dimples, and jet-black curly hair reminded him how much he missed his little girl. Placing his family in harm's way was not an option and it was then that he made the decision to cave.

Jacob's feet felt like lead as he walked toward the corner of the office where his safe was located. He opened the closet door, moved the extra suit jackets he kept for trial, and removed a portrait of The Ten Commandments, hand-lettered in calligraphy, expensively matted and framed in deep burgundy walnut.

How ironic! he thought, *I hid all my secrets in a closet behind the ten commandments of God. Just as God trusted Moses with his instructions, I am now about to hand over my secrets to a man I no longer trust.*

Jacob's mind raced as he knew that by opening the door to the safe he was taking a terrible chance. The black book that the safe hid contained all the dirty information he knew about each of his clients, stretching back to the days of his work as a public defender. For anyone to make it to the top in the city, that person needed the kind of damaging personal information on others that would discourage them from coming for him. Since Jacob did not want a digital trail, he held onto it with the hope of using it if anyone turned on him, but it had not occurred to him that he might need to defend himself from Clifford. Now, he wished he had gotten rid of the book along with their friendship. He knew that if he opened the safe, he had no control over how Clifford would use it. And yet, if he refused....

After glancing quickly over his shoulder to ensure that Clifford couldn't see his hands move, Jacob turned the dial on the safe.

"5—9—1------there," Jacob mumbled under his breath.

As he peered into the safe, he noted the pocket-sized journal in the back, on the right-hand side under some papers. On top, a black .40 caliber Glock handgun glimmered. He had purchased it after the Brian Nichol's courthouse shooting in downtown Atlanta in 2005, and as Jacob picked up the gun to move it, he suddenly found his hand—as if of its own accord—gripping the handle tightly.

Jacob knew handing over the book would give Clifford power over him, but he had to protect his family. Wild thoughts raced through his mind, *Why had he been so stupid? Why hadn't he destroyed the book when he had the chance?* This moment seemed like karma to him, as what he had intended to do to others, Clifford was now doing to him.

However, Clifford could not be allowed to blackmail him. He had come too far to be stopped by a greedy police officer who had once been a friend. With his hand still aware of the weight of the pistol, Jacob prayed. And then, he could feel the answer; *No, not that way.* He would have to find another solution.

———

Jacob had always hated drama of any kind. Even as a rebellious teenager, people had often called him the "cool dude" because he had a phenomenal ability to remain calm in even the most intense situations. When he had told Clifford months ago that he was going clean, Clifford had not seemed concerned. Although they hadn't talked since, the parting had felt casual, and Jacob had allowed himself to believe that he could go on to the next chapter of his life unencumbered by the old.

Jacob couldn't wrap his brain around what would happen if Clifford really told Rachel about their former collaboration. His shoulders ached with the effects of the adrenaline that coursed through his body, and he was surprised by the level of betrayal he felt at Clifford's apparent willingness to destroy his life. If he was honest, he could admit that he hadn't been a particularly good friend since he had immersed himself in law school. He realized he hadn't spent much time thinking about how hard it must have been for Clifford to flunk out and then to have gone on to become a police officer, while Jacob went to work in the Public Defender's office. It had seemed like a relatively small sin they were committing, because it was abundantly clear to everyone that the criminal justice system was broken, probably beyond repair, and at least this way, they could assure their own professional success.

Jacob's knuckles turned red as his left hand gripped the steering wheel while he stared mindlessly at the road before him.

"How could I have been so careless?" he

yelled, as his right hand slammed against the center console. The gesture caused his vehicle to swerve momentarily, and he nearly hit a black Volkswagen in the adjacent lane. The driver of the other car honked at Jacob, lowered his window, and screamed, "You fucking moron!" while gesturing with his middle finger; Jacob paid him no mind.

It seems everybody is fucking pissed in this damn city, he mused, as his thoughts turned to his wife.

Damn you Rachel, if you had appreciated the life I worked so hard to give you, our daughter would have done the same.

He knew that even now, there were many women who would love to be in Rachel's position. It was common knowledge that Jacob had been one of Atlanta's hottest bachelors before his marriage. When other guys fell head over heels chasing after girls, it was the reverse for him because he had worked his ass off to have the life he wanted. Now, it seemed that his family and the life he created were spinning apart in every direction.

He needed a plan, and fast. There was no way he was going to let Clifford destroy his family. As he drove onto the I75 North highway, he loosened his tie and lowered the temperature in the car. He needed to think things through properly, and he was grateful for the white noise of the surrounding traffic. Taking his usual route home, he got off the highway and as he drove toward Vinings he was reminded of the reason—his family—he could not allow the life he had worked so hard for to be destroyed.

He saw a couple with a little girl walking outside an ice cream shop; the man held the girl in his arms while the woman held a cone up to her mouth, obviously instructing her on how to lick around the outside without knocking the scoop off the cone. He remembered when things had been this good with his own family, though that felt very long ago. Then he passed three teenage girls in short shorts and tank tops with their arms entwined; the girls were giggling so hard they were almost doubled over, but as they walked up the sidewalk, listing from one side to the other, Jacob could see that the two on the outside were holding the girl in the middle up so she would not fall. *Might be alcohol*, he thought, with mild amusement. Then he remembered that he was going home to his alcoholic wife, and it did not seem so funny.

The garage door opened and Jacob drove his black Range Rover into the garage and parked next to his wife's 2018 silver BMW 750i. Once again, Rachel had parked terribly. Jacob wondered if she had been out drinking and driving again. It seemed the same story repeated itself endlessly.

After several attempts to wedge himself into the small space the BMW left open, he was finally able to park. Grabbing his briefcase, he attempted to exit the vehicle. The driver's door swung open, hitting Rachel's side mirror, nearly cracking it. As he surveyed the minor damage, he mumbled, "Maybe that will teach her to park better."

His knees cracked as he struggled to maneuver his 6'3" muscular frame between the two cars. Stretching his arms above his head, his eyes wandered in the direction of the garage door switch on the wall near the door. He decided to leave the garage door open in case he needed to leave quickly, a regular occurrence. The moment Rachel started nagging, Jacob would make an excuse to jump back in his car and return to the office. Now, all he could think about was removing his shoes, going down to the basement and watching SportsCenter till he dozed off.

As he approached the door, however, his frown turned into a slight smile. Wafting out into the garage was an incredible scent, and Jacob held his head back and took in a deep breath. As his eyes opened, he shook his head and whispered, "Whew, that woman has a gift." He was referring to Rachel's cooking, and as he entered the house, he wondered if he'd forgotten a special date: their anniversary or her birthday. He mentally reviewed the important birthdays and confirmed that the day was not one of those. Then, it hit him that he had been so occupied with Clifford that he had forgotten today was the anniversary of the day Rachel had agreed to marry him, though even then she had expressed some reservations about giving up her beloved job.

Jacob dropped his head in self-recrimination, simultaneously realizing that he had been missing Rachel lately. One thing he had always loved about her was that she was a beast in the kitchen. He'd missed her cooking, but more than that, he felt a sense of longing for the life he had imagined they would have; the connection, the sense of a shared partnership. He didn't know where that had gone, or if it had ever been there.

The smell of smothered pork chops, macaroni pie, and sweet potatoes combined into a wonderful fragrance signifying home, and he paused at the door to drink in the beautiful sight of Rachel as she stood over the stove tasting her food. He looked at her so lecherously that he wondered if that would make her feel shy. It had been a long time since he had come home to find her waiting for him. Things had changed since Sarah had left the house, and the stress from his law firm weighed heavily on their relationship. Jacob reflected that although he had thought the expensive gifts and big house he had gotten for her would be enough, his presumption turned out to be far wide of the mark. It was apparent that Rachel was not happy.

He needed something to take his mind off all the things that were swirling in his head, and he knew just the thing; hot and steamy sex. His thoughts quickly shifted from his problems to the red silky nightgown that gripped Rachel's hourglass figure. Although in her fifties, Rachel still had the figure and appearance of a swimsuit model and there and then Jacob couldn't decide which he wanted more; the food or Rachel. Each time she moved, her butt would shimmy in a way that sent a chill up his spine. He caught himself licking his lips and though it seemed she must be aware that he was looking at her, she did not turn toward him. Careful not to make a sound, Jacob quietly placed his briefcase and jacket on the floor, raised his dress pants and tiptoed toward the stove. When he got closer he realized Rachel was wearing headphones, apparently listening to music in her own world.

Slowly walking behind Rachel, he watched as her eyes closed and she raised the wooden spoon covered in sauce to her mouth. Jacob had just reached out his arms to envelop her in a hug when Rachel, suddenly realizing she was not alone, nearly knocking the pan of gravy off the stove. The gravy from the spoon splashed over Jacob's crisp white dress shirt but he did not care. Placing her hand over her mouth, Rachel quickly reached for a cloth to clean the stain; she knew how Jacob was when it came to his clothing. Before she could apologize, Jacob grabbed her and pulled her in close, causing her to drop the cloth on the floor.

Rachel threw her arms around Jacob's broad shoulders and he slipped his strong hands up her thigh. Suddenly, he felt the room grow warmer and couldn't tell if the heat was coming from the stove or her body. Rachel grabbed Jacob's tie, backing away from the stove and pulling him closer as he felt her begin to slide seductively against him.

"Damn! Somebody is happy to see me," he said as he struggled to keep pace with her flow. Then, another familiar scent hit him. This one, though, held entirely different emotional connotations; *Alcohol,* he thought, as he began to lean backwards in slight revulsion, but before he could break away, Rachel stuck her tongue down his throat.

Removing his hands from her body, Jacob gently pushed her away, scanning the kitchen for liquor bottles. It was not long before he eyes fell on a familiar sight.

An empty cocktail glass on the counter confirmed his suspicion.

"Dammit Ray, do you have to drink every single day?" Jacob grabbed his jacket and briefcase and walked away. *Shit, Shit, Shit,* he kept thinking as he made his way outside to his car.

Rachel stared at the food on the stove and her eyes began to water.

CHAPTER SEVEN

BIRD CALLS PENETRATED THE AIR as the park visitors enjoyed the unseasonably warm fall weather. Kids popped out intermittently from different directions, running and shrieking as they played variations on the game of tag.

Th park had been designed to facilitate the coming together of the diverse community around it, something people were determined to hold on to in this era when city officials were thinking of building industrial properties on public land. The scent of cheeseburgers, chicken and other outdoor goodies cooking on the various grills wafted through the air, signaling the importance of food in drawing people together.

Sarah and Kyle walked into the park and headed for the enormous Hickory tree that was Sarah's favorite spot, while people regarded them without curiosity. That was one of the features of the park Sarah appreciated most—people simply minding their own affairs. She wanted to be able to talk with Kyle in this peaceful place, away from other people, sitting on the grass in the shade where she could truly relax.

Sarah knew that the park these days was often filled with people experiencing homelessness, a thorny problem for which she had a compassion that was at odds with her desire for a peaceful afternoon. She recalled a day last summer when a man who was clearly suffering a break from reality removed all of his clothing, started chasing other park visitors around, and later stooped low to relieve himself in the middle of the park. Sarah had been there when the people from the Mental Health Crisis Team arrived, and she was hoping there wouldn't be a repeat of this kind of incident today!

Kyle had brought Salvatore Ferragamo, his two-year-old French Bulldog—who was usually called Sal—to share in the fun. Sarah often joked that Sal looked as though he were frowning and walked like a bully. The dog was indeed mean-looking as hell and people were afraid of him. At times, people would take one look at his face and choose to give him a wide berth. However, Sarah and Kyle knew him to be a gentle friend who was only aggressive in defense of those he loved (or in pursuit of a passing female dog).

Now Kyle remarked, "You seem distracted, baby... how are things at work?"

They paused as Sal did his business, and then, following the explicit dictates of park policy, Kyle scooped the result into a thin plastic bag prior to plopping it in the nearest garbage can.

Sarah waited until Kyle was through before she answered, "It's been really difficult lately."

They walked up the small hill to the base of the Hickory tree and Sarah shook out the blanket she had brought from the car onto the sun-dappled grass.

As they arranged themselves comfortably on the blanket, Kyle asked, "How so?" genuine curiosity in his voice.

"Well, it's a lot of work. That much I can tell you."

"Everything is harder when you're learning the ropes, and being a youth advocate definitely isn't 'a walk in the park,'" Kyle responded, grinning at his witticism as he shrugged and began to bring out Sal's frisbee, which seemed to be stuck in the bag. After a few jerks, the bag released the frisbee and Kyle threw it, shouting "Sal, fetch!"

Sarah replied, "Yeah, so much for the saying 'do what you love, and you will never work a day in your life.'"

"Girl, I don't know who came up with that cliché, but it's not true," Kyle agreed, patting Sal as he returned, before throwing the frisbee again.

Sarah glanced away and her eyes fixed on a group of teenage girls boisterously playing volleyball. A look of something like longing registered on her face. Kyle, who always paid attention, registered the look and asked, "You play?"

"No, but looking at the girls made me think of the kids that I work with." Sarah said. Indeed, seeing these girls, looking as though they didn't have a care in the world, made her think about the incredibly difficult lives of the young people on her caseload. Although Sarah knew that the world was starting to begin to understand the profoundly damaging effects of childhood trauma, there was still a long way to go.

"I guess watching the girls here makes me sad for my kids. I think of all the things they've had to go through, and it feels overwhelming sometimes."

Kyle looked at her, running his fingers lightly along her shoulder and down her arm in sympathy. "Baby you have to realize that change takes time. If you think about it, it's only relatively recently women have even been free to play sports in the way men have forever. Sports like football, baseball—exclusively male territory, and men like me—well you know we were expected to toe that line in a different way. You know; women were supposed to be making babies, caring for children, cooking, washing clothes and knitting their lives away—but society is changing, recognizing that we all have a responsibility for each other, and especially for children. We're not there yet, but it's coming."

Kyle could tell that although Sarah was listening, her focus wasn't fully on what he was saying and he asked,

"So, what's so hard about this case?"

Sarah looked at him, took the frisbee from his hands and threw it hard, sending Sal on a frantic gallop to fetch it. "This fifteen-year-old white girl is pregnant and she keeps getting thrown in and out of juvenile."

With his hand raised to his mouth and eyes widening, Kyle responded, "A white pregnant teenager! Say it isn't so."

It was a mock expression of amazement in which Kyle frequently indulged. Although his lightheartedness broke the mood of seriousness she felt the case deserved, Sarah appreciated his attempt to bring her out of her head, and she playfully slapped him on his knee, causing Sal to race back, dropping the frisbee between them and looking from one to the other with a serious expression, his tail wagging slowly back and forth.

Reaching over, Kyle rubbed Sal's slick white coat and murmured, "Calm down boy. No one's hurting me." Sal licked his nose and lay down on the blanket between them. Kyle knew that if another person had hit him the way Sarah just had, Sal would immediately have lunged at him, but Sarah was different.

Sarah continued, "Look Kyle, the little one doesn't belong in jail. She needs help. Tomorrow she has to go before a judge and I'm afraid the judge won't agree to get her the resources she needs."

Her eyes shifted downward at that moment and Kyle could see that she found her dilemma very painful.

"What is it you think should happen?" Kyle asked, as his expression became serious.

"I think she needs something way more personal than an institution can provide, though I don't know if she's ready to take advantage of whatever opportunity I find for her. Plus, this is my first time in front of this particular judge, and she has a reputation for being difficult." Sarah was well aware, from discussions with her peers, that Atlanta advocates dreaded appearing in this woman's courtroom.

"Yeah," Kyle replied, "helping people is not easy. Many people have learned not to trust others as a result of their experiences."

"I know, that's what the system often fails to address," Sarah reiterated.

"Well baby, you're absolutely right. Some people are just too scared to let down their guard to get the help they need. But having trustworthy people around can make a huge difference. And about that judge—of course sometimes people can be overbearing and think they know more than we do, but I have no doubt you will be able to advocate for what this girl needs."

Kyle looked at Sarah and continued, "I ran away from home when I was sixteen. When my parents found out I was gay, they tried everything to 'cure' me. Guess how my father did that? Dude literally made me attend multiple church services per week and constantly introduced me to more girls. When that didn't work, they said I was mentally ill or had a demon. They made it clear I was an abomination to them, and for a while I felt that way too. I even tried to see if I could change myself; it felt like it would be so much easier that way. But although I've always liked girls—and I can see that you're beautiful and appreciate that—it's different for me than it is for a straight boy. For a while I thought about just walking in front of a bus and ending it all, but I knew that wasn't the answer."

Sarah was staring at Kyle in shock, shaking her head softly. They wordlessly inched toward one another on the blanket until they were leaning against one another with their arms around each other. Gripping tightly, Sarah shook her head, exhaling audibly as she thought about how awful this must have been for him.

As if in answer to her thoughts, Kyle raised his sleeve to reveal the old scars marking his forearms. "Living in that home was hell and cutting was the only way I knew to cope with the feelings."

Sarah asked, gently "Was that when you were feeling suicidal?"

"No, I was cutting myself to let the pain out. I know people don't understand, but for some reason it helps."

Sarah interjected "I do understand—one of my psychology classes taught us it makes the body release endorphins, so although it might not be ideal, it's less dangerous than a lot of the other ways—like drugs or speed racing in cars—people find to deal with emotional pain."

"Well," Kyle continued, "when my parents found out about my cutting, they told their pastor, who came to the house and prayed over me in my bedroom. That was the last straw," he smiled, somewhat bitterly.

Wiping tears from her face, Sarah could only muster, "Oh Kyle."

"I had to make up my mind. I decided I would love myself and stand up for those who are treated unfairly. I was angry at the world and reached out to Pastor Fisher, who helped me get on my feet. He made the difference by believing in me. He allowed me to work at the church and live in the church parsonage. And he was actually the one who gave me the startup money for my boutique." Kyle's voice once again contained his characteristic cheerfulness, but Sarah was confused by this last bit of information.

Letting go of Kyle's hand, she asked, "Wait, the pastor who thought you had a demon gave you money for your business?"

Kyle smiled again. "No, silly. This was a different pastor. The pastor who thought I had a demon is my parents' pastor, Pastor Portland. He owns the mega-church over on the south side. He helps troubled teens but you can't be gay to get his help. He only deals with straight teens, and you have to come from low-income communities. He may be able to help the young lady you're working with."

Sarah shook her head vigorously, "No, I would prefer Pastor Fisher."

Kyle looked at the sky as if in prayer, "Well, that would've been nice. However, it's impossible; he passed away two years ago from complications of diabetes. He was a good man. I don't know about this Pastor Portland but he supposedly has a thriving teen ministry. He was given an award by Mayor Bottoms for helping former human trafficking survivors. So, even though he's not too fond of gays, he does do good for the community."

He paused before be continued, "My point is that, as you were saying, a human connection can change everything. But you can't save the world by yourself. You are not God."

They both laughed.

"You should bring the little one by the shop so we can get her some clothes she feels good in," Kyle said, rising to his feet, "Now let's get our butts moving and take this pup for a walk!"

CHAPTER EIGHT

S ARAH WAS IN A GOOD mood. Despite the challenges she faced at the office, she liked her job, although she had been slightly shocked to realize how much more there was to learn. However, she was starting to feel slightly less stressed dealing with Barbara, her still-difficult boss. In the time since she had begun working at the office, she had decided that Barbara might be a bit like a crab, someone with a hard exterior but soft insides. The woman often looked angry, but she could be warm on occasion, and really, Barbara was almost easy in comparison to some of the complex young people Sarah encountered in her work.

Sarah recognized that she had never before had to deal with a difficult teenager. Her only experience with kids prior to this job was the babysitting she had done for the children of her parents' country club friends, and although they could, on occasion, be a little bit bratty, mostly they were good-natured and happy to play in the pool while Sarah provided a little light guidance when it was time to transition from pool time to lunch time.

And Sarah herself had mostly been a pretty easy child, strong-willed but generally studious, though she could remember a couple of bad moments she had given her mother, and she now had a better idea about why her mother might have reacted as she had. Once in high school her mother had caught her sneaking a boy into the house in the middle of the night. Her mom's horrified look had made the boy shiver where he stood while Sarah shrank back against the wall as if hoping she could disappear right through it. Her mother had yelled "How dare you sneak a boy into your filthy room?!" She had then proceeded to tell the boy, Todd, that Sarah didn't like to clean, and that she still sucked her thumb when she was upset. Todd had looked from her mother to Sarah in shock—she was crying now, and, sure enough, sucking her thumb—before he fled the house like a dog with its tail between its legs.

The memory made her cringe. But although Sarah would never recommend that a parent use shame in this way to guide the actions of a child, she now understood—far better than she had when she was younger—how difficult it could be to try to convince a teenager to make good decisions, and how little prepared people are to be good parents in an ever-changing world. She made a mental note to tell her mother that the next time she saw her. Thanks to her job, Sarah was learning how to deal with those young people who had a great (and no doubt well-earned) distrust of authority.

As Sarah prepared to meet the needs of the newest young woman on her caseload, she reflected that too much of Aviela Scott's history had involved adults treating her like a piece of rag, according to the file notes Sarah read.

When police had found her stealing food from a local supermarket, they arrested her and discovered she had an outstanding warrant for prostitution. The judge gave her probation and assigned her to a group home. Now she was back in Judge Amy Grayson's courtroom, again for soliciting for prostitution. She was arrested when she helped set up a john to be robbed by her pimp. The pimp, of course, got away—and Aviela was arrested. She refused to tell officers the name of her pimp.

Although she was just fifteen years old, Aviela presented as older, no doubt a result of the harrowing life she had lived, and the criminal justice system appeared not to care that she was a juvenile. Aviela was seen as a delinquent and that was enough to place her behind bars, despite all of the research regarding brain development and the now-common understanding that the frontal cortex—responsible for making rational decisions—isn't even complete until one's mid-to-late twenties.

Now Judge Grayson, who would determine Aviela's placement, took one look at Aviela, who was wearing a ridiculously low tank top and ostentatiously chewing gum in her courtroom, and—deciding she would teach Aviela a lesson—sentenced her to three months in juvenile detention. Although Aviela had rolled her eyes at the judge, as if to convey how little she cared about the decision, Sarah knew juvenile was not the place for a pregnant teenager, and she pleaded with the judge to place Aviela in a new group home, one run by a group of women who had overcome similar odds. While the judge looked dubious, Sarah proceeded to tell her more about the group of entrepreneurs who had started *Free Soles*.

Sarah had learned about the group at a human trafficking conference she had attended in San Diego. She was blown away by how these women had turned their lives around and were now mentoring other young women. Each of the women had been a survivor of human trafficking herself, and the story of one in particular had caught Sarah's attention. She was a Chinese woman named Chenguang, with a body covered in tattoos, who had shared that she had been kidnapped from her parents at the age of ten. From that time, she had been trafficked through the sea to Amsterdam by the Japanese mob organization known as Yakuza, who had branded her their property and promised to slit her throat if she ever dared defy them. It was a tearful spiral down memory lane as Chenguang told Sarah about the countless times she had been drugged and made to sleep with as many as ten men a night. After about five years, she had been lucky enough to escape to the United States, where she sought refuge in the home of the creator of the women's group. When Sarah asked how it was that she had managed to get away, Chenguang explained that her captors had taken her to a nail salon, where the woman doing her nails had asked her, very softly and while looking at her intently, if she was ok. Although she had been terribly frightened, she had told the woman the truth—that she was being held captive—and the woman had nodded, and murmured that she would see what she could do. In fact, she had alerted the police, who had followed the car when it left the salon and soon after that, Chenguang was freed.

Sarah knew that there were agencies all over the world that were teaching hair and nail salon staff to recognize signs that might indicate one of their customers was being abused, or even trafficked, because the agencies had begun to realize that while women in these situations might never be taken to a doctor, or might be too frightened to talk if they were, the intimate environment of a salon might invite the kind of trust that provides an opening for abused customers to share confidences, and in fact this was proving to be true.

When Meia Sheling, the creator of *Free Soles* (so-named because the women had been freed not only in body, but also in spirit), told Sarah they had an Atlanta chapter of the organization, Sarah made it a point to get more information. Although Sarah wasn't sure if Aviela was ready to change her life, she figured that the women might be able to ignite a fire in Aviela and give her hope.

Sarah braked. The resulting squeal reminded her she needed to get her car looked at. Even though the 2010 Honda Accord, her high school graduation present, was still in good shape, she knew it needed some repairs and could only hope they would be minor. As the car slowed, Sarah remembered that Meia had told her there would be nothing identifying the group home, not even a mailbox, due to the need to keep its location hidden. *Free Soles*, and the women they sheltered, would be in danger of reprisal from the criminal trafficking syndicates against whom they battled. The women had received numerous emailed death threats, requiring them to change email addresses every four months. Sarah couldn't remember the exact driveway to enter, and since some of the other homes were also missing mailboxes, she reminded herself to note a landmark next time. Thinking she might have missed it, she swung into the next available driveway to turn around, but realized to her delight that she had stumbled upon the location after all. Slapping the steering wheel, she laughed out loud. "Isn't that lucky! I picked the right driveway by chance. Today is my day," she said with a grin.

Pulling around a curve in the steep driveway, Sarah drove up to the security gate. Meia had given her an access code so that she could come whenever she pleased, and Sarah murmured "the skies are bright for the ladies" to the smart looking female guard, who smiled and opened the gates to allow Sarah to enter. She pulled into the only available parking space and admired the building. She could see a bustle of activity, as the place was always busy during the day due to visiting counselors, teachers, and probation officers. As usual, she had called in advance to set this appointment to see Aviela.

As she placed the car in park, she felt a rush of pride in the work she was doing. Other activities might give her temporary pleasure, but the joy and excitement she got from helping people felt more truly meaningful than anything else she had ever done. Exiting the car, she glanced down briefly at her outfit; she had on the latest Evan Picone suit, which she had purchased from Kyle's shop. As she had imagined, Kyle's flawless taste in fashion helped Sarah look impressive, and Aviela had several times complimented

Sarah on how great—and how professional—she looked. Sarah had followed up on Kyle's offer to bring Aviela into the shop for a makeover, which the girl had very much enjoyed, and the excursion had allowed Sarah to introduce the two of them in a casual way.

Sarah now paused before walking up to the house and again appreciated the view of the place. The large ranch house was bright with its yellow paneling and vibrant orange shutters. A wrap-around porch with rocking chairs made the place look inviting. The twelve girls who lived there had planted a community garden on the side of the house, while the backyard housed a Peace Garden consisting of a waterfall with statues of children playing around it and a cross. A brick sidewalk surrounded the structure, with park benches strategically placed in a circle around the walkway. Each bench was painted a different color, with each color designed to indicate the current mood the girls might be in: red was for angry; yellow for happy; blue for sad; green for grateful, and orange represented curiosity.

The girls liked the benches because they allowed them to reflect on and communicate their emotions silently; they didn't have to discuss what they were feeling unless they felt inclined. Meia explained to Sarah that the benches symbolized how God hears our cries, even when we are silent. Sarah would often go to the Peace

Garden looking for Aviela, where the color of the bench she had chosen would give her a sense of how Aviela was feeling.

As she took another step toward the house, the door was flung open and a giant brown Labrador Retriever rushed out, immediately jumping all over Sarah's new suit and licking her face. It was Bud, the loyal pup who loved visitors. Bud was one of the therapy dogs who lived on the property to help the girls cope with anxiety. Chasing Bud was a light-skinned black woman who stood as tall as Sarah's mom. The woman wore a blue pantsuit and black heels and her smiling, freckled face gave her away as the homeowner, and Director of *Free Soles*, Meia.

"I'm sorry, Sarah. I tried to grab him."

"That's okay, Meia. I'm glad to see you!" Sarah said as she bent over to give the dog a pat on the head.

Mia slipped her fingers through Bud's collar and laughed, "I was actually on my way out the door when Bud heard you pull up. He nearly knocked me over in his mad rush to get to you."

"It's perfectly okay," Sarah responded happily, as she continued to nuzzle Bud, who gave an excited bark.

"Come right this way; Aviela's been waiting on you. I think she might be in the garden. She got up at six this morning to finish her chores early so she could spend more time with you. I can't tell you how much of a difference you have made in her life." She paused to greet a girl carrying a tray of freshly picked apples from the tree out back, and then continued, "I only wish all the girls had advocates as dedicated as you are."

As Sarah walked through the house, she saw that the other girls were completing their chores in the kitchen and gave them all a warm smile. She knew most of them, because she was known to be someone the girls could talk to, who loved to listen to their stories and never responded with disapproval.

She saw Hannah, a 14-year-old girl who had been brutally branded by a pimp who wanted the whole neighborhood to recognize her as his property. Hannah had finally escaped by lighting a fire while her pimp slept that burned down the house where he held her captive. She had barely escaped with her life, but she had been so desperate that she no longer cared. When the jury gathered to listen to the case, they all wept as they saw the burns Hannah had suffered, and in a rare outcome—likely due to her age when she came before the court—judged her not guilty of the charges of murder and arson.

Sarah then saw Hagar, a girl who had run away from her abusive home in California and ended up a sex slave in Las Vegas. Two men had seen her sleeping in a Greyhound station and disingenuously offered her a place to stay. Instead, they had driven her to Las Vegas, where they forced her into prostitution. When the

10-year-old had begged to be released, she had been beaten and transported to New Orleans, and finally to Atlanta, where she had been forced to work in massage parlors, providing men with hand jobs and other sexual services. She was rescued when suspicious neighbors prompted the Atlanta Vice Squad to serve a search warrant on the property. They had found Hagar hiding in the cellar along with several other young women, most of them immigrants. The police had taken her to the station, where they contacted Meia. Luckily, Meia had a great relationship with law enforcement. When little Hagar told the Atlanta police that she had run away from home because her father was molesting her, they investigated and found that Hagar had already reported the abuse to her teacher, but DFCS had investigated, her mother had successfully pressured her to re-tract the allegation. This kind of family response was sadly common in Sarah's experience.

Sarah passed Grey, Audrey, Sylvia and a couple of other girls, who all cheerfully called out "Hello, Miss Sarah." When Sarah stepped out into the backyard, she noted immediately that Aviela was sitting on the orange bench. It was the first time Sarah had seen her on that particular bench and she wondered what Aviela was feeling curious about.

"Hello there precious!" Sarah said as she walked up behind her and gave Aviela a hug. Aviela braced her right arm on the bench and attempted to stand but Sarah stopped her while placing her hand on Aviela's stomach, "No, no, now the two of you sit down." They both laughed and Sarah thought how good it was to see Aviela smile. More often, she saw Aviela brooding, and Sarah would worry over the health of the baby Aviela carried and try to think of things to cheer the girl up. On days like this, when Aviela's mood was already great, Sarah could feel herself relax.

"How are you doing?" she asked. "You feeling ok? You're looking big, girl! What did the doctor say about your delivery date?"

Aviela rolled her eyes and took a deep breath, "Whew, just about a month now. I can't wait; this little guy is seriously kicking my butt."

Sarah responded, "I know. Soon, you will have a little bundle of joy calling you mommy."

Even though Sarah had made the comment casually, she saw Aviela tear up, but she could tell that they were tears of joy rather than regret. "I can't wait for him to come out so I will have someone who is all mine," Aviela shared shyly.

Sarah was grateful that, in some places at least, women who got pregnant without the luxury of a solid partner could still find support and even moderate acceptance in the communities in which they lived. Of course, this had not always been true here in Atlanta, and while the stigma of unmarried motherhood was not entirely gone, Sarah knew that there were other countries in which a girl or woman who became pregnant outside of marriage was at risk of losing her life.

In these countries, unmarried women who got pregnant were likely to be thrown out into the street by their parents, regardless of whether the pregnancy was the result of a consensual relationship or rape. A recent news article had recounted the story of a father who had punched his pregnant 12-year-old daughter repeatedly in her belly until she fainted; she'd later died from complications arising from the attack. When the authorities asked him what had motivated him and whether he felt any remorse for his actions, he told them he'd had no choice but to appease his ancestors by eliminating "the abomination," and he evinced no regret whatsoever about killing his daughter.

Briefly giving silent thanks that this kind of thing was not common in the U.S., Sarah returned her attention to the tearful Aviela, who seemed to be deeply moved by the thought of her baby's unconditional love.

Sarah reflected on the fact that parenting was, of course, vastly more complicated than this, and that children actually need parents who love THEM unconditionally, rather than relying on children to fulfill their needs, but there would be plenty of time to discuss these kinds of things after the baby was born and Aviela had gotten used to being "on duty" 24/7, Sarah thought, smiling fondly.

Aviela gently leaned against Sarah, resting her head lightly against Sarah's shoulder, as if she could feel her thoughts. They watched as birds flew back and forth, sipping water from the fountain, basking in the shade provided by the large trees and relishing the cool breeze that carried the scent of the leaves turning on the trees that rimmed the garden.

Aviela took Sarah's hand and placed it on her bulging stomach. "He only moves around when he feels safe. Like now, it's as though he wants to come out and say hello."

Sarah could feel the little thumps hit her hand as it rested on Aviela's stomach. She rested her head affectionately on Aviela's and said, "Well, you both are safe now. Thank God for how he is watching over you both." Sarah wondered what the father of the baby was doing and was tempted to ask Aviela about him. It was kind of a forbidden topic with the teenager however, and since Sarah did not wish to spoil the mood, she refrained from asking. Still, she could not help but feel angry with the father, whoever he was; his absence robbed him of an incredibly important and beautiful experience, while denying Aviela the support she needed and deserved from him.

Aviela, meanwhile, had lifted her head from Sarah's shoulder, and now said, somewhat tentatively; "I don't mean to be rude Miss Sarah, but I don't believe there is a God. Because if there is a God ... why would he let this happen to me or the other girls?"

Sarah nodded reassuringly. She was glad that they were discussing this topic, as Sarah felt it would help Aviela—especially at this time in her life—to feel supported and held by a power greater than herself.

Sarah let out a huge sigh as she saw that Aviela's tears had begun to flow once again as she said "I don't want my baby to go through everything I've had to deal with."

Sarah was at a loss for words. She knew that there were many reasons why people expressed doubt in God, and one of them was that He often seemed to be absent when there was pain around.

After gathering her thoughts, Sarah removed her arm from around Aviela and turned to face her.

"Well. First of all, I want to thank you for being honest with me. It means a lot. And I want you to know it's definitely okay to have questions about this. It is hard to understand why bad things happen, and it's reasonable to feel as though this must mean there is no God. I'm not going to try to convince you that there is a God, but I will tell you what I believe: I believe that we are put on earth to try to learn to become our best, most compassionate, and true selves. I think that any time we act to make the world a better and more forgiving place, that's God in action. And yes, you're right. You did not deserve to be treated badly by anyone. No one does."

Aviela sniffled slightly and let her body relax again against Sarah's, nestling into her side as she realized that Sarah was not going to berate her for saying she didn't believe in God.

Sarah continued softly, "I believe God sent you to me, and I believe we are all God's children. It's our responsibility to make sure God's children are well taken care of and loved." Sarah saw that she had gotten the youngster's attention and was prepared to continue when Aviela looked up at her with her big blue eyes and asked, "Does God like mixed-race children too?"

Startled by the question, Sarah responded, "Of course, sweetie, what do you mean? God loves all children. We all come from God!" She paused; *I wonder if this is why Aviela was sitting on the orange bench today... .*

But Aviela continued, clearly in the throes of strong feeling, "That's not what my father says. He calls black people bad—says they are nothing but trouble. When he lost his insurance job and we had to move to Decatur, he said Affirmative Action was the reason he was pushed out of the job he'd for twenty-eight years. Then he started fighting with my mother and things at home got really bad."

Sarah looked at Aviela and sensed a confession coming, "Honey, is that why you ran away?"

Aviela sat bolt upright. "What?" Aviela sounded totally surprised. "Oh, Miss Sarah I didn't run away... My father kicked me out! He was furious when he found out I was going out with a guy from school—he tried to pretend it was because Gerald was older—he was 17 and I was 15 at the time—but I heard him tell my mom he would never allow his daughter to date a..." Aviela paused, and then said, so softly that Sarah could barely hear her, "He used the N-word, Miss Sarah...." Aviela kept her eyes on the patterned paving stones that edged the garden paths. Sarah didn't move. Afraid to break the mood that had allowed Aviela to share this obviously devastating confidence, she gently inquired "What happened?"

Aviela smiled sadly and said, "Well, of course we weren't going to stop seeing each other just because of some stupid reason... so we tried to be careful, just saw each other at school or met up after school on the days he didn't have football practice... I'd tell my mom I had to stay after to study, and he'd take me out for ice cream or we'd walk along the river and hold hands and talk about what we wanted for our future. We had one class together... we'd sit near each other and write notes... silly stuff, but he really was amazing—he cared about my feelings, what stuff I was interested in, what I was going through—we'd even talked about getting married once we were both done with college." She stopped and sat up, her face hardening.

"What is it?" Sarah asked, watching the shift, trying to imagine what it might portend.

"We'd just had our six-month anniversary when my dad must've gotten suspicious, because he went through my backpack and found some notes we'd written. He flipped out, told me he'd call the police and tell them Gerald attacked him when he tried to break up our relationship. He asked me, 'Who do you think the police are going to believe?' and I knew he was right. They'd never believe us.

Gerald said he didn't care—we could at least talk at school, and he'd wait for me until I was out of high school and on my own, but I know my dad; I didn't want to risk it, so we stopped seeing each other."

Aviela stopped and shook her head. "And it just went downhill from there."

"What do you mean?" Sarah asked. *It didn't really make sense—if the kids had stopped seeing each other...?*

But Aviela just shook her head slightly as if to indicate it was too much to talk about. Contemplating all that she'd just learned, Sarah placed both her hands on Aviela's shoulders and said, as warmly as she could, that her father's viewpoint did not reflect on her at all...that she was glad Aviela had finally been willing to tell her what had happened, and Sarah said how sorry she was that Aviela had had to deal with such an awful situation.

Sarah didn't want to leave the conversation on this note, however, so she said encouragingly, "And honey, although you don't get to control what happens to you, you choose how you want to respond—and your response will affect how much of that hurt passes on to your baby—and how hard you're willing to work to keep that from happening. Because there really isn't any formal training on how to be a good parent; most people learn to parent from the way they were raised, and too often, they are just trying to survive, so unless they understand how their experiences have wounded them—and how to heal from that—they risk inflicting the same kinds of harm on their children, even when they don't want to. That's why *Free Soles* has classes on understanding trauma, and why it's so important that you take advantage of all they have to offer, because it's pretty hard to be a calm and loving parent if you're feeling alone and afraid."

Sarah could tell she had gone on too long—this topic of healing from trauma was near and dear to her heart, and she needed to remember to give Aviela bite-sized chunks instead of her entire self-taught curriculum. Sarah mentally shifted gears and asked, "So, how do you want to spend the rest of our time together?"

Aviela got to her feet, face turned slightly away from Sarah, and asked—as though she, too, were glad of the change of topic, "What're we gonna have for lunch? I'm hungry!"

Sarah knew it was important not to press for more than Aviela was ready to give, so she stood and said "Mmmm... I was thinking we should call Kyle and see if he wants to meet us for lunch. What do you think of that?"

"Sounds good to me," Aviela replied, "I'd eat anything at this point!" She smiled, obviously pushing whatever dark thoughts she'd had back into the far reaches of her mind.

Sarah wished she knew the rest of the story, but when Aviela linked her fingers lightly in Sarah's before slowly waddling in the direction of the house, Sarah was reassured. Aviela was beginning to allow her to see underneath the layers of protection she'd built when dealing with the craziness in her home, and out on the streets. Sarah felt a flicker of euphoria rise up inside her, and knew—beyond a shadow of a doubt—that she was doing the work she was meant to do.

CHAPTER NINE

I T WAS A CHILLY AFTERNOON, and after checking in with Aviela at *Free Soles* in the morning,
Sarah had asked Kyle if he wanted to join the
two of them for lunch downtown. He'd suggested
they go to the Vietnamese restaurant next to
his shop, which he swore made the best pho in
town. He greeted them each with a warm hug
as they met outside the restaurant. Sarah had
been impressed by the easy rapport Kyle established with Aviela from the moment they met. Of
course, his stunning looks didn't hurt, but there
was also something so down-to-earth and *real*
about him that Sarah could understand why
Aviela felt so comfortable with him, and getting
together had become a fairly regular event in
their calendar whenever they could all arrange
it.

While they waited to be seated, Kyle asked
Aviela teasingly why she hadn't been back to his
shop since their last visit, managing to convey

without saying so just how precious he found her. Aviela grinned and responded in kind, telling him that the last outfit he'd given her had made the other girls at *Free Soles* laugh, and not with admiration.

It was clear from the way the restaurant staff greeted Kyle that he was a regular, and the three were swiftly ushered to a spacious table by the window. A waitress brought a stainless-steel teapot from which Kyle poured steaming, fragrant tea into small ceramic cups already on the table. They each took a sip and Kyle, noticing Aviela's expression, kindly said; "It's ok to put sugar in it if you prefer," handing her the large glass jar with silver top and flapped spout from amongst the various soy and chili sauces grouped at the end of the table.

As Sarah and Aviela surveyed the menu, Kyle offered to answer any questions they might have, but the waitress had returned almost instantaneously, obviously expecting that they would be ready to order. Sarah and Aviela shook their heads, admitting to being totally out of their element and in need of more time.

The waitress appeared slightly impatient, but Kyle smiled and assured her that he would assist them while she attended to other customers. He then inquired whether Aviela and Sarah were in the mood for rice or noodles, hot soup or something more like salad and what kind of meats they liked, and when Aviela asked, with evident admiration, "How do you know about all these dishes?" Kyle told her that his mother's family was from Vietnam, and that his grandmother had cooked many of these foods for him when she was alive.

"Does your mom still make them, now that your grandmother has passed? Aviela asked.

"I don't think so," Kyle told her, "but I don't actually know."

Aviela's confusion showed on her face; she knew he was gay, but Kyle had never shared the story of his parents' reaction to this fact. Kyle explained that he had not been in touch with his parents for a very long time, briefly described their horror when he'd told them, at age 16, that he was gay, and how his life had changed forever once he had recognized the conditional nature of their love for him. He said he'd left home when it became clear they had no interest in ever changing their views, and talked about how cold and friendless the world had seemed for some time afterward.

Aviela's eyes had not left Kyle's face while he talked, and at that point she murmured softly, "Yeah, I know what that's like."

Kyle already knew from Sarah some of what Aviela had been through, but he knew it was important that she be allowed to tell as much of her story as she felt comfortable sharing, so he simply invited, "Tell me."

Aviela seemed pleased at his interest in her

past, but her quick side-glance out the restaurant window suggested hesitation about what to share, and before she could begin, the petit waitress had returned, holding her pen over the order pad as she glanced at Sarah and Aviela to see if they had finally made up their minds.

When it was clear no decisions had been made, she said sharply, "You take time, okay!" as she walked abruptly away, causing Kyle to offer, "Hey, why don't you let me order for you?"

Sarah glanced up from the menu, giving Kyle a dubious look.

"What, you don't trust my choices?" he asked.

Aviela and Sarah looked at Kyle leopard-print shirt, red pocket handkerchief and black vest, and then back at each other before bursting into laughter.

However, sensing that his prompt to order might have been sparked by the waitress's reaction, Sarah agreed, "Yes we better order; we don't want Kyle's friend mad at us with that stank attitude!"

"She doesn't have an attitude," Aviela said quickly, the certainty in her voice surprising her companions.

Sarah turned in her seat so that she could face Aviela, her wrinkled brow telegraphing her puzzlement.

"Why do you say that?" Kyle queried from across the table.

Aviela looked down at the table before saying quietly, "She's scared."

As they sat for a moment, absorbing this incongruous statement, Sarah and Kyle both sensed that something momentous was happening, even if they didn't know what it was.

It was evident that Aviela had inferred something the older two had not perceived, and they were curious to know what it was. They stared at Aviela in anticipation, but though Aviela was gratified to have their rapt and respectful attention, the circumstance was not one she would have chosen to demonstrate her extensive knowledge of the world of the streets.

She shook her head slightly and leaned forward to whisper, "Check out the hostess. Most hostesses are younger pretty girls, right?"

Their glances traveled to the cashier's station near the doorway, taking in the eagle-eyed matriarch surveying the restaurant, receiving and cashing out patrons and inquiring about their enjoyment of the meal.

Sarah agreed, but protested, "Well maybe she's the owner?"

Kyle nodded his head.

Aviela exhaled heavily; "Of course she's the owner."

Kyle's and Sarah's expressions indicated they were both still clueless. Aviela picked up her menu and pretended to read, avoiding eye contact with the waitress, who was only two tables away. Sarah and Kyle followed her lead.

As the waitress moved away, Aviela leaned forward and whispered, "The next time she comes over, look at her shoes," as she took a quick glance in her direction.

"What is it with you young people and shoes?" Sarah asked.

Aviela shook her head, and then continued, "If you knew you were going to be on your feet all day, wouldn't you wear comfortable shoes? She's a waitress and she knows she'll be on her feet all day, but she's basically wearing cardboard— that's all those little thin shoes are, no better than cardboard—on her feet. Nobody's that poor— she could get sneakers at the thrift store for a few dollars that would at least cushion her feet. No. Somebody doesn't want her to run."

Kyle realized that despite having been here many times over the years, he had never really *looked* at the waitresses or thought twice about the fact that they often seemed tired, with perhaps a hint of sadness lurking below their surface smiles. If he *had* thought about it, he would likely have assumed this was because they had such a physical and demanding job.

As he pondered this, the waitress reappeared at their table. Looking a bit wilted but with all traces of annoyance carefully wiped from her face, she asked the group, "You order?" Kyle nodded "Yes," while trying not to stare too hard at her feet. She wore no socks, and as his eyes followed her legs, he noticed slight bruises on both ankles and a small cut beneath the left one which looked fresh.

Consumed with what might have caused this, Kyle momentarily forgot that he'd been put in charge of ordering until Sarah covered for him by ordering for herself, "Um, Hmmm ... I'll try the egg rolls and a bowl of your chicken noodle soup."

Aviela put down the menu, saying, "And I think... Kyle should just pick something for me."

"At least somebody trusts me!" Kyle laughed, "my young friend and I will have Banh Hoi Thit Nuong and Banh Hoi Ga Nuong."

Kyle looked at Aviela, and told her; "Don't worry, it's just Vietnamese for sliced pork and chicken served with fancy rice noodles." Aviela let out a sigh.

The waitress finished scribbling down their orders and extended her hand to collect the menus. The interchange had given Sarah a chance to look at the woman with this new awareness. Her eyes caught a burn on the back of the woman's writing hand. *Nothing unusual,* Sarah thought, *she works near hot plates and food, that could easily have come from an oven, except, it looks more like a cigarette burn... and her feet, and those marks on her ankles... .* Suddenly Sarah found herself thinking that the owner's sharp surveying gaze might be more

than the usual attention of a restaurant propri-
etor who wanted to make sure guests were well
attended to.

As the waitress walked away, Kyle and Sarah
looked at Aviela and Kyle leaned across the table
toward her and asked; "You mean to tell me ...?

"Yes, she is being trafficked." Aviela interrupted. Sarah looked at Aviela and asked, "How
did you know this?"

Aviela replied simply, "It's pretty easy once
you've been there."

Sarah put her arm around the girl next to her
before saying intently, "I think you're right, and I
know a detective who can look into this."

Aviela nodded seriously, and then shifted in
her seat and changed the subject, asking, "So
Kyle do you have any matching outfits for me
and my baby?"

Kyle put this hand on hers and stated playfully but with an avuncular warmth, "You know
I'm going to be the baby's godfather, right?"

Aviela responded, "Well I don't know about all
that; are you going to help me change his dia-
pers?"

CHAPTER TEN

THE SUN SPREAD ITS BRIGHT orange glow over the horizon as the wind blew softly, rattling the tree leaves lightly against one another and making a harmonious sound. Sarah and Rachel made their way down the walking trail, enjoying the scenery in one of Atlanta's most popular attractions, Piedmont Park. The city skyline reflected off the lake located in the center of the park while birds chirped in the trees. It was an exquisite fall day.

As the women walked stride for stride, they swung their arms back and forth, periodically checking their respective Fitbits for the number of steps taken and calories burned. Occasionally, passing joggers would force them to move to the right of the trail. It was hard for Sarah to keep up with her mother's long legs. Plus, her mom was a regular at the park. She loved to run. Sarah hated running.

"So, how is everything going down at the office?" Rachel inquired. Sarah slowed her pace to gather her thoughts. She wondered if her mother was really interested, or just wanted to pry into her business. She did not want to tell her mother how hard it was to see broken families every day.

"It's okay, I guess. It's not that I expected it to be easy. It's just more intense than I thought it would be. It seems never-ending, the number of people caught in these kinds of situations, and I guess I just don't understand why so many poor people also suffer from so much physical and sexual abuse. It seems as though they're cursed!"

Rachel turned her head to look at Sarah for a moment before letting out a short, sarcastic laugh and shaking her head.

Sarah stopped dead in her tracks. "What's funny Mother?"

"Well, its sounds like you think abuse only happens in impoverished neighborhoods, or to poor people."

"I never said that, Mother. But since working there I haven't witnessed any rich white people walking through our doors asking for help!"

"That doesn't mean white or wealthy people do not experience abuse. They may just handle it differently. You ever thought about that?" Rachel exclaimed

"Did you ever see wealthy families in the system when you worked as a child advocate?"

"Well, I've certainly known well-to-do families

in which abuse was occurring, though of course their wealth makes it easier to hide it—" Rachel paused thoughtfully and looked away, across the lake where ducks floated peacefully atop the barely rippling water. "I guess now may be the time to tell you why I became a child advocate." Rachel pointed to a nearby park bench and invited Sarah to have a seat. Sarah took a deep breath. She knew when her mom tried to make her comfortable, it usually meant bad news. Her mind raced to worst case scenarios. *What could she possibly be about to share? Was she adopted?* Yes, Sarah needed to sit down. Her legs were beginning to shake. The sound of her heartbeat echoed in her ear drums.

"Sarah, you know that I was a child advocate and that I loved it. But I never told you why I dedicated my life to helping abuse survivors. You see, I myself am a survivor of abuse. I was abused by my uncle."

"Your uncle?" Sarah asked as she leaned away from Rachel in order to be able to better see her face. Standing suddenly, Sarah cried out in shock. "Oh, my God Mom! Please tell me it's not Uncle Henry!"

Rachel rose to her feet and said, gently soothing her; "No, honey. Uncle Henry would never do such a thing. Please calm down and sit with me."

Sarah reluctantly returned to the park bench. Taking her mother's hand, she could feel Rachel's sweaty palm, and she suddenly felt faint as she glanced over and saw the strained look on her mother's face.

"It was my Uncle Darrell." Rachel was now holding her head down.

"When I was 13, I had already begun to become uncomfortable with the attention from the men and boys that came around me. Girls at my school were jealous because I was so much more developed; one of my classmates even scribbled a letter, asking me to please stop stealing the attention of other boys. They really hated me." Rachel burst suddenly into loud laughter.

"What's so funny, Mom?"

"I was just remembering one day in 8th grade, between classes, when I went into the restroom and saw three of my classmates stuffing their chests with padded cloths. I laughed. I couldn't help it, they looked so funny, but this really earned me the ire of these three girls, who were some of the school's most popular. But my biggest problem wasn't at school. It was at home."

The conversation was making Sarah terribly uneasy; she realized she was sitting stiffly, perched on the very edge of the bench, her lips pressed tightly together. It was hard for her to maintain her composure, but she knew how important it was for her mother to be able to tell her about this, so Sarah tried consciously to relax her muscles, breathing in slowly and softening her face so that when she looked again at her mother, the tense look had been replaced by a warm and understanding expression. Sarah briefly gave thanks that her experience with the children she worked with had taught her to listen to even the hardest tale without betraying shock, or anger, or any other emotion that would keep the person from feeling able to tell the whole story.

Rachel continued "Everyone loved Uncle Darrell. He was the first one in the family to graduate college and start his own business. When he lost his business from a combination of bad investments and his gambling problem, he asked my father and mother for assistance. They agreed to help him get on his feet. I think they only did it because he had children. At first, Uncle Darrell's family of four coming to stay with us looked like a blessing. I finally had two cousins to play with. Maggie, Freda, and I would skip rope games or braid Barbie's hair while giggling about the boys in our classes. But when I would go out with my friends, Uncle Darrell would go out of his way to tell me I looked amazing in my 'pretty little dress.' Then, on other occasions, he would draw me close into a long personal hug when his wife and kids were not around. I never saw him hug his wife or daughters the way he did me."

"Mom, this sounds just like so many of the stories I hear from young girls who come into our office!" Sarah sighed. She couldn't believe what she was hearing. Just as Sarah was about to ask her mother a question, a small Dalmatian puppy interrupted their conversation. The puppy sniffed and licked Rachel's feet. As Rachel smiled appreciatively at the warm affection, the spotted black and white puppy stood on his hind legs and tried to climb into Rachel's lap, almost as if he were attempting to console her. Just as she reached down to caress the puppy, a sturdy-looking white woman dressed in athletic gear approached, quite obviously out of breath, and grabbed him up in her arms, "I'm sorry, he just loves people."

"No, it's okay." Rachel responded. They both watched as the woman walked away with the puppy, who whimpered and wriggled in an attempt to escape again.

Rachel continued her account where she'd left off. "Our parents taught us to respect and trust adults, especially those close to us. It was easy to trust Uncle Darrell. He seemed like he couldn't hurt a fly. He would call me his 'angel' and invite me to sit on his lap while he playfully tickled my ribs. I loved when he took me to the store for ice cream and tucked me into bed. I felt like his own daughter. At times, I felt like he treated me better than his own two girls, and although I wasn't totally comfortable with that, I have to admit that a part of me liked feeling special. I never got that from my mother. Your grandmother worked long hours and your grandfather rarely came home. So Uncle Darrell and his family made everything easier for Mom and Dad."

Rachel paused for what felt like an age. It was obvious she was having a difficult time discussing her past. However, Sarah knew sharing her experience gave her mom an opportunity to heal. Even if it was hard for Sarah to hear, this was her mother's journey, and Sarah touched her mom's leg to let her know she was there.

Rachel looked at Sarah, as if to ascertain how this tale was affecting her daughter.

Then she continued, "I remember it like it was yesterday. The abuse started on a sunny afternoon when Uncle Darrell picked me up from school. He drove me home, humming my favorite song under his breath while sharing a laugh when I told him he sounded awful. When we got to the house, he invited me into his bedroom. He said he had something to show me." Rachel paused again, dabbing with her handkerchief at the tears which had begun to form. Then, she continued.

"I followed him. I had no reason to believe he would hurt me. When we were inside his room, he slowly locked the door and moved toward me, softly telling me how beautiful I was, how much he loved me. I was confused by his words, and asked what he'd wanted to show me, but before I could make sense of what was happening, he began to touch my breasts, unzipping his pants with his other hand. I shielded my eyes and tried to move away from him but he grabbed my hand and told me that he wanted to show me how to be a woman. He began to touch himself and then he placed my hands on him. I tried to scream but nothing came out. My mother only told me not to allow strange men to touch me, she never warned me about family."

Rachel placed her face in her hands. It was hard for her to continue. Sarah looked around the park to make sure no one was eavesdropping on their conversation. She tried to calm her mother. "Mother, it's okay. You don't have to do this if it's upsetting you too much. We can just go home."

"No, Sarah! You need to hear this and how it affected me." Rachel exclaimed. "I kept on begging him to stop but it was as if he had turned into a beast with fire in his eyes. He was hurting me and he kept on making these weird noises that I had never heard before and he sounded like an animal." Rachel sniffed and looked at her daughter. "Sarah, I could not do anything at that moment. The fragile little world that I had built was destroyed by this man whom I had regarded as my shield. When he finished with me that first time, he warned me that bad things would happen if I told anyone."

Sarah had often heard this kind of thing reported by the children with whom she worked. She'd always felt sympathy for them when she heard it, but it was different hearing it from her own mother. Now Sarah could feel her body suffuse with fury at the man who had dared threaten her.

Rachel's usually carefully applied mascara was streaked across her cheeks, but she continued her story and Sarah gripped her mother's hand supportively.

"The worst part was, when I went to the police and told them what he did to me, no one believed me. The detectives said there was no evidence of it and they did not want to destroy my uncle's good reputation. My father and his side of the family said I'd made the whole thing up. Thank God for your grandmother. She stood by my side the entire time. But I felt so bad for telling. It tore the family apart, and I've always known that I was the reason for my parents' divorce.

Sarah and her mother sat quietly after her mother finished; Sarah was processing what she'd heard. Finally, she asked tentatively, "Why didn't you tell me about this before today?"

Her mother responded slowly, as though thinking through her answer as she spoke. "Well, honey, when you were young, it didn't occur to me. I thought it would hurt you unnecessarily, and I didn't want you to feel as though the world was an unsafe place. And, of course, there was, and still is, a stigma around acknowledging abuse—there's a tendency to 'blame the victim' and as I said, I was already blaming myself."

Rachel sat back against the slats of the bench

and sighed. When she spoke again, it was with a tone of resolution.

"Now, though, I've begun to realize that abuse thrives in secrecy—and when I hear your passion and dedication around helping the kids, it reminds me of when you were a child. I don't know if you recall, but as a little girl you would sit in front of the television and watch programs that featured starving children around the world. You would even ask me to send your allowance money to help those children."

Rachel smiled at Sarah and continued, "After that happened to me, I promised God I would spend the rest of my life protecting other children. But when your father came along, I got caught up in living the life he wanted us to live, and although I continued to give money to various charities, I didn't stay involved personally. I've missed it... more, I guess, than I even realized."

Rachel used her fingers to wipe the residue of her earlier tears from her eyes, further smearing the black makeup across her face. As she saw the color on her fingertips she laughed. "Look at me. I'm a mess. I'm so sorry. You came here to get advice from me and I gave you... probably a lot more than you ever wanted to know."

Sarah thought that this was both true, and not true, because as hard as it was to think about, she was glad to understand more about what had made her mother the person she was, and she felt good at the thought that she might, through listening, have helped in some small way. She responded, "It's okay, Mom," and though she could hear a hint of ambivalence in the way the words came out, she knew it was almost totally true.

Rachel further mused "I chose security because the world was always an insecure place for me. But Sarah, I'm telling you because I did not want you to think this only happens to the poor and underprivileged. This happens whenever someone allows his *or her* (because although it is more often men who abuse, abuse is not exclusive to men) desire for power to blind them to the harm they're doing to someone vulnerable, whether that vulnerability comes from the person's youth, or their fear of being unloved, or whatever it may be."

Rachel shifted so that she could gesture toward the open-air rotunda at the park's entrance. "See that fountain over there? After everything that happened with my uncle, my mother knew that I was traumatized—though they didn't use that word, even in the social service field back then; she made a huge effort to help me see myself as a strong and valuable woman. Momma always told me 'inner beauty rises up and blesses the world like the water of a fountain.' She modeled for me how to be a strong woman, and told me that one day I would be a hero for some girl out there. That's why I read you the story of the great Amazons who were so feared and respected by men and gods that they were left alone."

Sarah continued to listen to her mom with full attention, though she was finding herself slightly unsure where she was going with this. She'd always known her mother to be someone whose stories took some turns before Rachel eventually arrived at her point.

"Now, I guess this will be part of the way I help women around me—telling you my story, and helping you understand that abuse comes in many different forms; it's certainly not limited to poor people, and, as parents, we really have to think about the way we raise our children. I've realized over the past few years that although your dad and I got a lot of things right with you, we also passed on some of our own insecurities— I know you've felt as though your dad didn't support you because you chose to go into social services, but it comes from his worries that you would struggle the way that he did."

"And I know I did the same thing sometimes— I let my own fears about what *might* happen get in the way of recognizing that you are an individual with your own life to lead. I guess I'm coming to understand better how important it is that we trust your judgement about what's right for you. You know that we'll be here if you need us.

"I do know that Mom, and I'm so sorry you

had to go through all that," Sarah murmured softly.

They hugged, and Sarah felt her mom's arms tighten around her, and then, as her mother let her breath out, Sarah could feel her relax. That, for Sarah, was a sign of a fighter; someone committed to learning from and overcoming life's many challenges.

CHAPTER ELEVEN

I T WAS LATE AND AVIELA should have been sleeping, but instead she was slipping out the back door into the chilly night air, carefully closing the wooden door behind her and catching the screen door before it could snap back against the frame as it liked to do.

Her back ached and she slipped one hand under her swollen belly as she padded across the patio to where the row of rocking chairs sat, clutching the bulky wool blanket she'd draped awkwardly around her shoulders with her other hand. Cold nipped at her legs through her fleece pajamas and her troubled thoughts roiled inside her mind.

Settling herself—as comfortably as she could in her current condition—into the nearest of the rocking chairs, Aviela tucked the blanket in around her legs before relaxing gratefully against the back of the chair.

She looked appreciatively at the sliver of

moon visible over the tops of the trees surrounding the yard and her thoughts turned to her parents. She wondered what they were doing right now. Her father might just have gotten home from one of his lengthy days as a long-haul trucker, expecting his wife to have a delicious home-cooked meal waiting for him. Whatever she made, however, was never good enough. He always found reason to criticize, leaving her mother in a perpetually anxious state, and both of them unhappy.

Aviela could picture her mother as she'd seen her so often, kneeling devoutly in front of the little statue of the Madonna she kept in the guest bedroom with a rosary in her hands, while she prayed for the holy Mother of God to be with her daughter.

As Aviela thought about her mother, she could feel her throat tighten. Now that she was about to have a baby herself, she wished more than ever that she and her mother had been closer. It wasn't that she thought her mother didn't love her, but too many times she had taken her "duty" as a wife more seriously than her duties as a mother; something Aviela vowed never to do to her own child.

The chirping of the frogs mating in the little grove of fruit trees in the backyard echoed through the clear night sky. Light from the stars and moon gave the place an almost eerie look, though Aviela always felt peaceful here.

As if the baby inside her could feel what Aviela was thinking, he kicked. Aviela felt him and smiled, patting her belly.

Then her mind wandered back to the lunch she'd had with Sarah and Kyle the day before, at the little restaurant near his shop. Aviela hadn't expected to like the food, but she enjoyed trying new things and she loved the time they spent together.

And, although it had been extremely painful to take one look at the waitress and recognize that she was almost certainly being held captive, it had been amazing to share this knowledge with Sarah and Kyle, and to have them take it, and her, so seriously.

Aviela reflected that the truly special people in the world were the ones who took time to really listen.

Her mother, dad, and pastor—even the other social workers and advocates she'd had over the past year—seemed only to know how to talk. They never listened at all; or, maybe more accurately, they never tried to *hear* her. They ignored what she was saying and focused instead on what they wanted her to do, and finally Aviela had stopped telling them anything.

Until Sarah.

No adult had ever spent time just getting to know her the way Sarah did. It was a big part of what Aviela had loved about her relationship with Gerald—that sense of being heard and understood and cared about—but it had not occurred to Aviela that adults could be interested in listening to what she had to say, except when it suited them, and usually in order to ensure her compliance.

Deep in thought, Aviela's fingers tapped a steady rhythm on the arm of the rocking chair. It helped soothe her mind so she could focus on the positive thoughts amidst the—significantly more numerous—negative ones. She knew she could not afford to give in to fear, because that would take its toll on her baby, her doctor had warned.

As Aviela continued to tap and to rock gently back and forth, her eyelids grew heavy and she could feel herself drifting toward sleep. Suddenly a loud *crack* came from the house behind her. Momentarily alarmed, Aviela tried to rise to her feet, holding onto the rocking chair for balance. Belatedly, she recognized the sound as that of the screen door slamming and identified the figure coming toward her.

"Dammit, Nicole, Aviela said quietly, "You almost sent me into labor!"

She heard the other girl utter a little gasp and smiled. Nicole ought to know the dangers of sneaking up on a pregnant woman

"Shhhh, I'm sorry," the girl said, as she assisted Aviela back into the rocking chair before taking the seat next to her and leaning over to pat Aviela's stomach. "Hey bud, I hope everything's okay in there? Don't you come out just yet."

That was the nature of Nicole. She could be funny when she wanted to be and odd at the same time. She'd arrived at *Free Soles* just a few days after Aviela, but she still hadn't seemed to really settle in.

Nicole was fourteen years old, African American, tall for her age, and athletic. Many of the other girls avoided her because they thought she was a chatterbox, and she could be. She always believed that she had something to offer, a word of advice or a fun story to tell. With her neatly trimmed short hair and muscular physique, she was an attractive tomboy who had been rescued in a human trafficking raid three months earlier by the Metro Atlanta Task Force. Initially, they'd sent her to an area group home, but she kept running away—something many girls in the system had in common.

Eventually, Nicole had been fortunate enough to hear about *Free Soles*. She'd been on the street, begging for money, when one of the program's off-duty staff members approached her. The woman had taken the time to ask Nicole about her situation, and then offered to take her to a safe home, describing it—and the people who ran it—in glowing terms. But Nicole had initially refused to go anywhere with her.

The woman had seemed totally unsurprised, and, after telling Nicole she understood her lack of trust, she'd given her $10 for food and a card with the number of the home. She said she was often in the neighborhood, so if Nicole wanted to go with her another day, she would be happy to take her whenever she was ready.

It had taken another few nights on the street, but early one morning soon after, Nicole was waiting on the same corner when the woman walked up to her and asked, with a big smile, "Is today the day?" And Nicole had answered, somewhat hesitantly, "Yes."

Nicole now straightened her sweatshirt and said to Aviela,

"I'm sorry, but I couldn't sleep either. I've been watching you for a while and seeing you get up most nights and I've wondered where you go."

Aviela, who knew that the other girls at the home were curious about her movements, sighed.

"I come here to clear my head and count my blessings," she replied, somewhat curtly, hoping to forestall further questions.

Nicole looked intently at Aviela, apparently uncertain about whether to believe her or not. Although counting one's blessing was definitely encouraged at *Free Soles*— focusing on 'the positive' had the power to change the way the girls felt about their current lives, and consequently the choices they made about their futures—the trauma they had experienced meant this was not always easy.

Aviela kept rocking in her chair. Hoping to shift the conversation away from herself, she asked, "Where did you say you from again?"

"Decatur. The bad part, not the good part," Nicole said as she sucked her teeth.

Aviela observed, in order to keep the conversation focused on Nicole; "You don't look fourteen."

"Everyone tells me that," Nicole said, laughing out loud. She took a quick survey of herself and seemed to like what she saw. Then she glanced back at Aviela, who was in the process of preparing to go back inside, but Nicole started talking again;

"Oh, I thought maybe you were worried like me."

Aviela sat back down, confused, "Why would I be worried?"

"I mean. What are they going to do with us after we have our babies? If you haven't noticed, there are pregnant girls here but no babies... and what happens to the girls after they have their babies?" Nicole asked, lowering her voice. Even though most of the group officers would be resting at that time, Nicole appeared to feel it was best not to proclaim her fears too loudly as she continued,

"I heard a rumor..."

Aviela could not understand what Nicole was saying. She was slightly curious, but she did not want to sound eager so she muttered a little "mmhh"

Nicole took that as an invitation to continue, "I mean, once I got pregnant, he got ... I mean they got rid of me. Maybe it's like that."

Aviela could not keep silent, "I don't understand. What are you saying?"

Nicole did not pause, "I've heard those people at DFCS do some pretty bad things!"

Aviela was getting irritated by Nicole's uncharacteristic reluctance to talk specifically, and she demanded to know; "What bad things?"

"Well, they take your baby when he's born and put him in the system. Bam... You don't get to see him again for life. They say the baby belongs to the state...."

Nicole's voice trailed off as she saw the look on Aviela's face and seemed to realize that her words might have hit home harder than she'd intended;

"Whoa, easy now; remember, I said it's just a rumor," Nicole said, reaching over and putting her hand on the arm of Aviela's rocking chair.

Aviela could feel sweat gathering in her armpits despite the cold as she thought about what Nicole had said. She could not imagine anybody taking her baby away from her, and the prospect was terrifying. "So, did you ask anyone about this rumor Nicole?"

Nicole hesitated before answering and then

said, "No... because... why would I trust them to tell the truth? I was so happy when I first got pregnant. But then I realized things weren't going to turn out the way I'd hoped. But I knew my baby would be special."

Aviela planted her feet on the ground to stop the rocking chair. Sitting forward on the edge of the seat, she turned and faced Nicole. Her lip protruded as she tried to control what came out of her mouth. She counted to three to gather her thoughts—a trick Sarah had taught her to prevent her from saying whatever she felt like—before asking, as neutrally as she could,

"You wanted your baby to have problems?"

Nicole smiled as she understood Aviela's question, "No, not special like that. I mean special as in sent from God special."

Aviela, recalling the conversation she'd had with Sarah in the Peace Garden just a few weeks back, replied reassuringly; "Well it seems like—if there is a God—all children must be sent from God, don't you think?"

"I guess," Nicole responded, though her eyes glanced down as she considered for a moment before saying, "I just wished my child's father felt that way."

Aviela didn't respond immediately. The remark showed how much they had in common, and Aviela found herself becoming curious about

Nicole's past, prompting her to ask, "So, your child's father... he doesn't want the baby?"

"My child's father is a liar and a hypocrite!" Nicole blurted out, though she looked as though she regretted speaking the minute the words left her mouth.

"He sounds like *my* child's father," Aviela responded miserably. She was suddenly too sad to talk anymore, and she got up to go back inside but Nicole stood also and stepped in front of Aviela, blocking her way.

"Aviela, I'm scared. What are we going to do once we have our babies? I mean, I have no family and the one person I trusted let me down. There really isn't anyone I can depend on."

Aviela suddenly recognized so much of herself in Nicole that she impulsively grabbed Nicole's hands, "I don't know either... I don't know what we should do. Maybe we should pray... it can't hurt... maybe God will help us," Aviela offered.

"God?" Nicole spat out vehemently, "It was God who got me into this mess. If I wasn't trying to please God I would never have gotten pregnant. My child's father told me God wanted me to have sex with him, and I thought maybe he was right, but when I got pregnant, he said I had to get rid of the baby." Nicole snatched her hands away from Aviela and started walking toward the garden. "I will never trust a pastor again."

The words rang in Aviela's ears. "Wait, what's

that about a pastor?" Aviela asked, rushing to keep up with her.

Nicole brushed her question away, saying "Never mind. I don't want to talk anymore. I need to be alone."

CHAPTER TWELVE

THE NOVEMBER MORNING WAS CRISP and clear as Sarah left her apartment and walked to her car. When she'd told her supervisor the previous night that she would not be in the office first thing, Barbara had looked irritated, but Sarah was committed to spending actual face-to-face time with the young people on her caseload, even if it meant, as it frequently did, that she had to stay late in the office doing paperwork.

As Sarah adjusted her seatbelt, she noticed that she was actually feeling... happy. After a long time of feeling as though every day was about preparing for the future—getting through school, working crazy hours at jobs that didn't feed her emotionally just to pay bills—she was finally in a place where, although her case list included more families than she felt she could serve well and there was always too much paperwork, she also had moments like this, when she felt she was using her gifts to help others, and that they were making a difference.

Sarah was truly enjoying the challenge of figuring out how to support Aviela so that the young lady could heal from the abuse of her past and become the best mom possible to her son, while simultaneously preparing for a satisfying future for herself.

When Sarah had left Aviela after that first meeting, she'd been struck by the extent to which the teen's trust in the world had been broken.

So many people and systems had let Aviela down, from her family, whose unhappiness and disfunction had left her vulnerable to being preyed upon by whoever had gotten her pregnant and abandoned her; to the legal system, built on archaic and disproven beliefs about brain function and what's actually effective at preventing people from committing crimes—and rather than offer help to society's vulnerable—sorts humans into 'worthwhile' and 'worthless' categories, which contributes hugely and needlessly to recidivism and general misery, not to mention vast sums of wasted money; to the DFCS system that had passed her from advocate to advocate, ensuring that she could not bond with anyone. It really was staggering to contemplate.

Sarah had known she would need to rekindle Aviela's ability to trust in something, and this effort had required relocating the young girl to

Free Soles and then ensuring that she spent quality time with Aviela.

Sarah started the car and began driving toward the group home. As she drove, she turned up the volume of the car radio and bumped to the beat of the jazz music that played through the speakers. Jazz was not usually her kind of thing. She'd loved Soft Rock since she was a little girl—to her mom' chagrin. Sarah remembered her dad buying CDs of the famous rock bands at that time, and how her mother's face would register disapproval; Rachel wanted Gospel and Soul to be the only genres in the house. For a time in high school, Sarah and her friends had flirted with the idea of starting up a girl band.

When they began to research the cost of new guitars, space, drum set, and other instruments, however, they decided to let the idea drop since they were sure that their parents would not support them. *Who knows, maybe Aviela might like to learn to play an instrument after she gives birth*, Sarah thought, considering some of the myriad opportunities she wanted to provide for the girl as she pulled into the *Free Soles* driveway.

Sarah reached over to the passenger seat and grabbed the gift bag she'd brought to surprise Aviela with. It contained a teddy bear wearing an 'I love Mommy' T-shirt, and lots of things she might want while in the hospital, including cute socks and lip balm and a stylish hair band to keep her hair out of her face when she was in labor. Sarah wanted her to feel loved and supported when she went to the hospital to deliver the baby, so that the experience would be as comfortable as it could be and she would have people there with her, including herself, Kyle, and Meia, in lieu of her parents and the baby's father.

As she approached the door, Sarah could hear Bud barking on the other side of it. Meia swung the door open holding Bud by the collar. It was difficult to determine sometimes, Sarah thought with amusement, if Bud was actually a therapy dog or a guard dog, but once he saw it was Sarah he sat and began wagging his tail.

"We were just about to call you...."

"What's going on? Is everything okay?"

"I'm afraid not. It appears Aviela has run away."

"What? Why? What happened?"

"We're not sure, but one of the other girls, Nicole, can tell you what she knows. Go get Nicole please," Meia instructed one of the aides.

"This is not good; she's about to have the baby!"

"Yes, of course," Meia affirmed.

Sarah was totally caught off guard. She couldn't imagine what might have possessed Aviela to leave; she had seemed to be doing so *well* these last few weeks... so positive, connected... looking forward with excitement to being a mom... It didn't make any sense.

"Come in, Sarah, and have a seat. I know this is a lot to take in. You don't look well," Meia noted as she took in the ashen look on Sarah's face and wrapped her left arm around Sarah's shoulders.

"Bring me a cold towel," Meia instructed a passing girl.

She walked Sarah to the conference room and began to dab her face with the towel she was brought.

She was interrupted by a soft voice coming from the doorway. "Yes, Ma'am?"

―――――――

Sitting at her desk at the office that afternoon, Sarah discovered that the officer who had taken the report had categorized it under "runaway juvenile," instead of "missing person." Sarah was furious. This meant the police department was not going to put effort into looking for her. Sarah was coming to understand the harsh nature of this system wherein police officers saw people as either "good"—and therefore worthy of concern or "bad"—in which case they were summarily dismissed, or treated as subhuman.

Sarah knew the job was incredibly complex, but she did not excuse those who seemed to have lost their ability to empathize.

She wanted to catch up with Aviela before she got hurt, because whatever her reasons for running—and Nicole's explanation had failed to provide much information beyond that she, Nicole, had told Aviela that the state was rumored to take the babies belonging to the girls staying at *Free Soles* and keep them in the system—she was not safe on the streets.

It was hard for Sarah to believe Aviela would have been taken in by this false rumor, but she couldn't imagine what else might have caused the girl to leave *Free Soles,* and when she'd told Kyle that Aviela was missing, he agreed that nothing they'd seen in Aviela's recent actions had suggested she was about to run.

Letting out a huge sigh, Sarah scanned the office for someone from whom to seek advice. However, everyone looked busy and buried in their own cases. She would not blame any of them if they could not make time for her because all of her colleagues were weighed down with disasters of their own. Looking at her office phone, she thought about calling Detective Askew, but didn't want to risk Barbara overhearing her conversation. Barbara frequently tried to discourage those under her from what she called "going above and beyond," and Sarah had learned not to say anything if she was intending to do pretty much anything beyond filing necessary paperwork.

Sarah found Barbara puzzling; she could not

understand why anyone would work in social services who did not actively *care* about making a difference, and she often wondered if Barbara realized the extent to which she had given up—if she ever thought to stop and look at the picture of herself on the wall in her office. It was sad to think that this once-beautiful woman, brimming with life and positive energy, had been reduced to a grouchy old bear who basically drained the life out of the job instead of encouraging the advocates to do their best for the clients.

Sarah grabbed her cell phone and headed to the ladies' room, listening to see if anyone else was inside before dialing the detective's number. The propensity to snoop was one of the key features she'd noticed about the people who worked in her office. They seemed to love to share juicy news with each other, and while Sarah liked to know what was going on, she hated this practice because the bad news always spread faster than the good, and this seemed unproductive to Sarah.

Disappointment washed over her as the call went straight to voicemail. "Hello, Detective Askew, this is Sarah Clarkston. When you get a moment can you call me? One of my clients has gone missing and I need your assistance." After leaving her numbers, she hung up the phone. She had not talked to him since she'd called to thank him for recommending her for this position, but finding Aviela seemed like a job for a detective.

Sarah returned to her desk to think of her next move. Then, while waiting for Askew's call, she decided to look back through Aviela's file to see if she had missed anything that might help her figure out where Aviela had gone, or why.

The office was really too noisy for her to focus and Sarah would have loved to get out of there and find a place where she could think. However, she knew that she could not, because most of the important information was located on the DFCS computer filing system, which was not available via the internet once she was out of the building.

Sarah had hailed this as a smart move when she came. She appreciated that the county government limited the ability to read the records to those within the building so that they could keep track of who accessed them. At the moment, however, Sarah didn't think it was such a great idea.

As she browsed through the records a second time, she noticed the names of the different caseworkers who had been assigned to Aviela's case. She ran her thumb across the screen and counted four advocates assigned in the two months prior to Sarah's getting the case. Sarah hadn't known enough about the system when she first took on Aviela's case to know how unusual this was, but now she recognized it as very odd.

I wonder why they didn't keep her with one person? No wonder she had an attitude when I met her at the Detention Center, Sarah thought.

Often in an office, there was a case that no one wanted to touch. In the advocate office, the problem cases concerned kids who were particularly temperamental, or who tended to escape from their juvenile or foster homes whenever they got the chance, creating additional work for their advocates.

As she continued to review the material, Sarah noticed that Detective Askew had worked on a couple of Aviela's previous runaway cases but had closed all of them with insufficient evidence and without charging her with any crime. Well, at least when Sarah did get the chance to talk with him he would already know who Aviela was and he might have some ideas about where she could be.

This case had become somewhat of a mystery to Sarah, and the part of her that loved puzzles began to emerge, allowing her to bury some of her feelings in action.

Sarah knew that the degree of loss, and—if she was honest with herself—betrayal she was feeling was considered "unprofessional," but she didn't care. She knew that the relationship she and Aviela had developed had made a difference in the way the girl had begun to see herself and the potential for her future, and Sarah was totally stunned, and even a bit hurt, that Aviela would have done this.

"Where could she be?" Sarah wondered for the umpteenth time as she slowly tapped her pen on the table and began to search her mind for any minute detail that might give a clue as to Aviela's whereabouts.

CHAPTER THIRTEEN

A s SARAH NEARED HOME LATE that afternoon, she saw a large crowd in the street near her apartment. Exhausted after searching for Aviela through every avenue she could think of, Sarah wondered what this gathering of people signified. She looked around, and then up at the sky, in the hope of seeing what was amiss. Perhaps there would be smoke, which would indicate that a building was on fire. However, there were no firefighters. Sarah had once wanted to become a firefighter, and a friend told her that girls couldn't be firefighters; when she had repeated this story to her mother, Rachel had laughed out loud and told Sarah that she could be anything she set out to be if she only had belief in herself. *Yeah, as long as I don't want to be a social worker, right Mom?* She thought.

Sarah continued to drive slowly, but when she attempted to get into her apartment complex, she was stopped by two police officers.

"Sorry, Ma'am, you can't park here. This is an active crime scene," one of the officers informed her. She saw that they had cordoned off the place with their traditional yellow tape. Pointing out of her vehicle over the officer's shoulder, Sarah stated,

"But I live in that building right there."

"Sorry, Ma'am, you'll have to park elsewhere and walk to your apartment."

Sarah sighed and pulled out again, turning to park where they had indicated. Obviously, they would not budge and she was too tired to argue with anyone at that moment. The officers watched as she parked before turning back to their tasks. After switching off her ignition, she left the car and began walking toward the crowd. She spotted her nosy neighbor, Mildred, standing at the group's edge. Normally, Sarah would have avoided her at all costs because Mildred was a gossip and much of the information she passed around was known to be false, but today Sarah wanted to know what this gathering of people was about. When Sarah reached her, she asked, "What's going on, Mildred?" Mildred whispered in reply, as if unsure whether she wanted to be associated with this, perhaps the biggest bit of gossip she had ever been party to; "I found a body!"

"What are you talking about, Mildred?" Sarah said, moving closer and turning to face the older woman properly.

"There was a girl lying dead in the woods behind our building." Mildred continued, as she wiped a tear from her face. *She can be emotional sometimes: emotional and heartless,* Sarah thought.

"Oh, my God! Really? Who was she? What was her name?" Sarah shot off questions like an automatic weapon. She did not like to be in the dark at any time, and especially when it concerned a dead body lying at the back of their building.

Mildred responded, "I don't know. I've never seen her before, but she was a young white girl, and I heard someone say it looked as though she'd recently had a baby!"

Sarah's throat closed as her thoughts connected at lightning speed, her earlier fears about Aviela's disappearance, and the sense she'd always had that Aviela was afraid; afraid of saying too much, acting as if someone might want to hurt her ... Sarah reached into her purse, extracted her phone and, shaking now, scrolled through her pictures until she found the one she wanted; a photo she and Aviela had taken one day at the park. Remembering the day, she was flooded with emotions as she looked at the lively, bright-eyed teenager staring back at her. Her brown hair, blue eyes, and infectious smile hid so much pain.

Sarah noticed how close Aviela's face had been to her own as they had posed for the selfie. It was amazing how much a smile could conceal.

In the background, a red cardinal perched on the park bench. It was almost as if the bird wanted to be in the photo. They had both laughed when they'd looked at the picture and realized they had been photobombed by a bird. The picture was the only one Sarah had of Aviela looking happy, and it had been taken less than two weeks before.

In her heart, Sarah was certain that Aviela would not have run away from the mentoring program. Since arriving at *Free Soles*, Aviela had started studying for the GED, attending child-care classes, and she'd even begun talking about starting her own nonprofit for young mothers. Aviela would not have gone so long without com-municating with her; they had been in almost daily contact for the last couple of months.

Sarah became aware that she did not actually want to know the identity of the girl found in the woods; her instincts told her it was Aviela, and Sarah took a moment to compose herself.

Finally, she held out her cell phone, Aviela's picture on the screen, "Is this the girl they found in the woods?"

Mildred peered into the screen and then up at Sarah before saying reluctantly,

"I think that would most likely be the girl."

Sarah found herself shouting, "Don't think, Mildred! I need to know; why do you think this is her?"

"I found the body while I was out walking my

dog," Mildred responded. Her bottom lip began to quiver as she continued to describe what she had seen. "I saw a little part of her face. Little thing is wearing a light blue sweatshirt stained with a lot of blood and her head all twisted up in the wrong direction. Dear God! How do you know her?" Mildred asked suspiciously as she wiped her tears again, shaking a bit from the gory details she had described, and the idea that Sarah might be connected to her. She had never seen Sarah with the girl, and, at least at this moment, looked as though she wouldn't have wanted to.

Sarah whirled and ducked under the crime scene tape, running toward the woods before being cut off by a group of officers.

"Get her out of my damn crime scene!" a man yelled from just outside the woods as he talked with another officer who seemed to be placing evidence into a thin plastic bag

Sarah looked at the man and saw it was Detective Askew. As the officers were trying to escort her away, Sarah struggled and began screaming, "Detective Askew! Detective Askew!"

When Detective Askew saw it was Sarah, he ordered the officers to release her. Sarah turned around and ran back, forcing her phone into the detective's face.

"Is this the girl? Is this the girl? Answer me, dammit!" She could tell by the look on Detective Askew's face that the body found in the woods was Aviela. Sarah doubled over, a sound part way between a scream and a whimper finding its way from inside her body. Detective Askew grabbed her arm to keep her from collapsing entirely, and motioned for the paramedics to come attend to her.

When Sarah came around, she saw Aviela's body being loaded into a hearse. She jumped out of the paramedic's truck and ran towards the hearse screaming "WAIT! WAIT! Can I see her, Detective, please?"

Detective Askew asked the coroner to unzip the body bag; there lay Aviela's frail, defenseless body. Sarah burst into tears, but as she looked at Aviela's corpse she noticed that there was an unexpectedly peaceful look on her face, and Sarah reflected that at least she was no longer in pain. Sarah eyes slowly surveyed her, noticing that, indeed, her stomach was flat. Shocked, Sarah placed her hand on her heart to slow it down. Her breath slowed and she felt faint again. She braced herself against the stretcher. "Wait a minute... where is the baby?" Sarah thought out loud and was about to ask Detective Askew when a loud commotion was heard in the woods near the crime scene. "Detective Askew!" Several voices were calling.

"Wait here, I think they found something," he said to Sarah and hurried off.

Sarah ignored his command and ran behind him. When they got to the woods they saw one of the officers holding a crying baby boy. The officer reported, "We heard movement in the woods and when we checked, we found this baby concealed in the bush. She must have hidden him from her killer."

Detective Askew took the baby and summoned the paramedics. Then he looked at Sarah and told her she would have to leave. She was standing in an active crime scene. Sarah asked, "What will happen to the baby?"

Detective Askew responded, "I'm not sure. First, we'll get him examined at the hospital. No telling how long he's been out here."

Sarah let out a sigh. She had no energy left. The tears flowed down her face. She had never felt so much pain. It seemed as though she had been making so much progress with Aviela. They had been planning for her new motherhood and anticipating how much fun it would be to watch her little boy grow up. Now, she was gone. A paramedic showed up and retrieved the baby from Detective Askew.

The detective put his hand on Sarah's shoulder and told her gently, "Go home and get some rest, Sarah, I'll take it from here."

He began to walk away but Sarah grabbed him by the arm and said, "That's the girl I came to the police station to tell you about, but you would not listen, now she's dead. Dead!"

Askew looked at her seriously before saying in a low tone, "I'm sorry Sarah, but we can't save them all." He turned and walked back toward his detective car. Sarah started to follow, but she was cut off by two uniformed police officers. "Sorry, lady, but you can't come near the crime scene! Please back up or we will have to arrest you," one officer barked.

"Chill, Robocop! I'm not hurting your fucking crime scene!" Sarah thought to herself, but was too afraid to speak it aloud.

Instead, she stood in silence and watched the hearse drive away with Aviela's body. She walked back to her apartment with her heart buried in pain. Blaming Detective Askew had not stopped her from feeling terribly guilty. She should have found a way to keep this from happening.

Sarah needed to talk to Kyle, but she waited until she was inside to call him, because she knew that his sympathy would cause her to lose all semblance of control, and she was right.

When Kyle answered her call with a cheery "Hi baby!" she had burst into the kind of wracking sobs that made it hard to breathe. She was crying so hard he couldn't even understand her, although he quickly figured out that Aviela was dead.

In shock himself, he'd closed the shop immediately and driven right over. By the time he made it to her apartment, Sarah had sunk down against the wall of the hallway between the kitchen and the bathroom and was hugging her knees with her arms. Kyle helped her up from the floor and half carried her to her bed, lying curled around her and holding her while she told him what she knew, and they cried together for hours until he had to go home and get Sal, who was waiting unhappily to go out.

He brought the massive pup back to Sarah's after a walk, and Sal eagerly bounded over to Sarah where she lay on the bed. She was able to give him a few pets before Kyle rejoined her on the bed and they all finally drifted off to sleep.

The next morning, Sarah called Barbara to say she was sick and would need the day off. Barbara had tried awkwardly to say how sorry she was about the loss of Aviela, but Sarah was beyond caring. When Barbara was done, Sarah thanked her listlessly and told her she would see her at work on Monday. And with that she ended the call.

Kyle was back after taking Sal out for a quick morning walk and bringing her a steaming mug of coffee. He sat on the bed with her and asked how she was doing. She could only shake her head; everything she wanted to say made her cry again, and he simply put his arms around her, sitting with her and letting the physical comfort do what words could not.

He'd made breakfast and brought it to her on the bed, saying, "Here you go baby, you need to eat something. Even though I know you don't want to, it will make you feel better."

He was going to go open the shop, but he asked her if she wanted him to leave Sal there with her, which she did, and he said he would call to check in on them later and, if she needed him to be there, he would close the shop and come back.

Laying her eyes on the perfectly arranged scrambled eggs, toast, and fruit salad, she barely heard what he said. She thought how glad she was to have him to share her memories of Aviela with, but she told him she would be okay until he got finished with work. Kyle grabbed his things and headed for the door.

When Kyle returned from work that evening, Sarah did not appear to have moved from where he had left her; she had not eaten more than two bites of her breakfast. After cooking more food and coaxing her to eat a couple of bites of stir-fried vegetables, Kyle convinced her to take a bath, while he took Sal out again. He was glad for the care Sal needed, as it helped him orient himself during this incredibly difficult time and he knew the exercise was good for him as well.

When Sarah came out of the bathroom, she said she felt a little better, but it was clear that she was still in shock.

Kyle got her back in bed and sat across from her in the only other seating available—the overstuffed armchair—and talked to her about other things, including a story about one of his favorite customers, a little old white lady in her 70s who liked to come into the shop and try on various outlandish outfits before finally settling on one—with Kyle's always enthusiastic assistance.

He had tried to make Sarah laugh, but to no avail. She managed a wan smile, however, and assured him she would be fine if he went home, and then promptly drifted off to sleep again. Kyle regarded her fondly. The tranquil look on her face made her appear younger. It was the first time he had witnessed her at peace. Sarah was always worried about something. After kissing her on the forehead, he made sure the covers were arranged just so before gathering himself to go.

As he turned to leave, a group of family photos on the fireplace mantle he'd never noticed before caught his eye. Kyle wasn't the nosy type but he was a bit curious about Sarah's past. They had talked some about her childhood, and Kyle knew that Sarah saw her mother pretty regularly but that her father was a successful lawyer who hadn't wanted her to work in the field of social work; he'd been so adamant about it that he'd refused to pay her college tuition unless she changed her major, which she had been unwilling to do.

One picture in particular caught his attention. It was a photo of Sarah as a child standing next to a man and a woman he assumed must be her mother and father. He thought Sarah looked just like her mother, except that she was not as tall, though he could see hints of her father's strong jawline in her current, grown-up self. He smiled at the way her hair was barely contained in her pigtails and her jeans seemed a bit too short. He was amused that she would display such a picture, until it occurred to him that this picture reflected the time before Sarah had been, essentially, estranged from her father, and it looked as though things had, overall, been pretty happy back then. With that thought, he left the apartment and locked the door behind him.

After Aviela's passing, Sarah felt like a zombie, barely able to remember what day it was. Living seemed challenging, and she supposed that simply dealing with the feelings of loss— without trying to stuff them or numb herself—was the best thing she could do at this point. She was stunned by the degree to which she missed the precious little being she had known for such a comparatively short while. Her whole body ached, and it felt as though there was a permanent lump in her throat.

Sarah realize that there would be many practical things to attend to if Aviela was to be given a decent burial, and she told herself sternly that she had to pull herself together.

First, she forced herself to contact the parents and tell them how sorry she was for their loss. While on the way to see them, however, Sarah realized that she was not at all sure she would be able to be compassionate toward these people, despite their having just suffered the death of their daughter. She could not imagine the kind of parents who would leave their little one alone on the streets as Aviela's parents had apparently done.

Sarah recognized that parents held many hopes for their kids, but that teenagers needed to become independent, even (especially) when doing so went against their parents' wishes. Many teens would smoke if their friends were doing the same. They would want to engage in sexual escapades if their friends said it was cool. Parents, of course, would want to intervene and redirect teens away from this potentially life-destroying behavior.

But no matter how narrow minded they might be about her dating an African American, how could that have made Aviela's parents abandon their daughter? Sarah wondered.

When she reached the parents' home, she found herself staring at another puzzle. By every standard, Aviela's parents were not as poor as she had envisioned they would be. The well-manicured lawn and flowers planted in the yard gave Sarah a sense the parents were hard-working people. She exited her car and walked up to the unremarkable ranch house located in a modest middle-class community nestled in the city of Stone Mountain. She didn't plan to stay long. The police had already made the death notification, but Sarah wanted Aviela's parents to know that she had been turning her life around before she was murdered. It was the only decent thing to do.

She didn't know how she would respond to them, however, knowing how they abandoned Aviela. But maybe there was another side to the story.

Before Sarah could ring the doorbell, the front door swung open. A slender, tired-looking white woman stood in the doorway wearing khaki pants and a tan blouse. Sarah immediately noted her resemblance to Aviela, and she wiped tears as she approached the steps.

"Hello, you must be Sarah," the woman said as she extended her hand. "I'm Sandy. Come in. I'll introduce you to my husband Bill."

Sarah walked in the front door and noticed the wide-open floor plan. The décor reminded her of something out of a home and garden magazine. "What a nice home you have Mrs. Scott."

"Thank you, and please call me Sandy," the woman invited, as they entered the living room space. Sitting on the sofa watching the news was a white man with reddish-blond hair and a ruddy complexion, dressed in faded jeans and a light blue dress shirt. As the two women rounded the corner, he didn't budge or even look in their direction.

"Honey, this is Sarah. She's Aviela's social worker."

"*Was* her social worker," the father retorted, staring fixedly at the T.V. screen. "Our daughter would still be alive, living in this house if she wasn't so damn hard-headed. I tell you when things started going bad. It's when she started hanging around with that nig...."

"BILL!" Sandy quickly interrupted

"Black boy, Gerald or whatever his damn name is." The father stood up abruptly, gave a quick glance at Sarah and stormed out of the room.

Although Sarah had gone in with her guard up, she felt her stomach clench momentarily as she withstood the impact of his predictable ignorance, her eyes impassively following his retreating figure.

"I'm sorry. Please forgive my husband. He misses her. He just doesn't know how to say it."

Sarah shook her head as she exhaled and did what she had come to do; "It's okay, Mrs. Scott. I mean Sandy. I wanted to stop by and tell you how well your daughter was doing before she passed." Sarah didn't want to use the word "murdered." It sounded too harsh. "I spent quite a bit of time with her these last few months, and it was exciting to see her begin to value herself, preparing to be the best mother she could be for her son—she was going to school, she'd identified a couple of potential career paths... I'm so sorry about your loss, and I thought you'd want to know," Sarah said softly.

"Thank you for coming to tell us this," Sandy responded with what felt to Sarah like sincerity.

Going by the way they dressed and spoke, it was obvious that lack of money had not been the primary issue here. *Surely they could have found a way to keep a connection with their daughter, even if she was making choices they disagreed with,* Sarah thought. She'd looked as they walked through the house and saw many crosses, along with images of Jesus around the table with his disciples. Sarah remembered an argument her parents had had about hanging Jesus pictures in the dining room. Her father was against it. He always said he did not want a white man getting credit for his own hard work.

As Sandy walked Sarah outside, she looked over her shoulder and quietly pulled the front door shut. She placed her hand on Sarah's arm and tried to hold back tears. "I apologize again for Bill. When he found out Aviela was pregnant with Gerald's baby he couldn't take it."

Sandy was now crying with one hand over her mouth. She dropped her hands by her side and stated, "I didn't want you to think we're bad people. We just wanted better for our daughter. Bill thinks Gerald didn't want the baby and had Aviela killed to avoid paying child support. He'd tried to get Gerald arrested when we first learned she was pregnant, but Aviela wouldn't cooperate. The detective we spoke with at the precinct told us he would speak with Aviela and try to get her to open up, but he never called us back. Just a minute."

Sandy reopened the front door, peering in cautiously to see if her husband was near. Then she reached inside, grabbing a business card from the table in the entry hallway and handing it to Sarah.

"Here's the detective my husband contacted and asked to bring charges upon Gerald. Things didn't work out the way my husband wanted. Look, I want to find out what happened to our daughter. Maybe you can contact this detective and see what he and my husband discussed. Just don't tell him we spoke. If my husband found out I gave you this information, he would..." Sandy paused and looked Sarah in the eye and continued, "well, he would not be happy."

Sarah thanked Aviela's mother and turned to leave. As she got to the bottom of the stairs, she looked at the business card. She nearly tripped over her feet as she read it. She turned around and waved to Sandy, hoping she didn't appear as flustered as she felt. Her pace hastened as she rushed to her car. Once seated, she lifted eyelids that felt unusually heavy as she peered through her lashes to see if Sandy had gone back into the house. Starting the car, Sarah inhaled and glanced at the card again. This time she read it slowly out loud: "Detective CJ Askew Badge 1971 Atlanta Police Department Special Victims Unit."

CHAPTER FOURTEEN

THOUGH ENGROSSED IN HER THOUGHTS, Sarah noticed that the black hearse had come to a stop. Unconsciously she moved a little closer to Kyle, and they exchanged a quick glance that carried a shadow of the pain they had been through since Aviela had disappeared.

As the pallbearers carried Aviela's casket to the grave site, several people gathered. Some people from the neighborhood where her body had been found had come to the funeral. Sarah knew that some might have brought their own kids to show them what happened to kids who did not obey their parents. As a Victim's Advocate, Sarah was beginning to see how years of unresolved trauma affected generations of families.

The families were so afraid for their children they tried to control them as a way to protect them, rather than show them the compassion that might have allowed the young people to feel accepted and to trust that they could come to the adults in their lives with their problems.

As a result, many children she worked with were distant and fearful, and she felt sorry for them. Sarah pressed her lips together and realized that she was feeling sorry for the children, but also for her own losses—of Aviela, of her father, and of the community she'd left when she felt that her father had let her down.

Kyle put his arm around her shoulder and Sarah could feel the softness of the cashmere coat against her face as she acknowledged his sympathy, brushing her cheek gratefully against his arm. She looked up at his face then; the stiffness there suggested that his thoughts might have traveled a similar path—there was nothing like death to make people think about their own mortality, and, by extension, their relationships, including both the positive ones and those that were not.

The small white casket in front of them was adorned with silver trimmings. In front of the casket, two men were placing flowers. There was one from the funeral home, and a lovely arrangement from the staff and girls at *Free Soles* as well as one that Sarah and Kyle had bought together.

Sarah was surprised to see Aviela's parents had purchased nearly half a dozen floral arrangements. The sight of the casket brought Sarah to tears. She quickly scanned the small crowd and noted that Meia had brought most of the girls from *Free Soles*, and though not all the girls were crying, there was a palpable sense of unease as they crowded close together; some of them held each other's hands, and each appeared to be considering not only Aviela's death, but their own vulnerability.

It was the kind of event that inevitably felt like something from a movie. Sarah tried not to think about how angry she was with Aviela's parents, but her hands got warm and sweat started to roll down her back nevertheless. Her temperature always rose when she got angry.

"How dare these people try to make it look now as though they'd been loving parents all along?" She thought. *That child needed you and all you did was judge her and try to control who she loved!*

Sarah was not particularly religious, but she'd never doubted that God loves children. When she had heard as a child the old wives' tale that storks made and delivered babies, she had simply laughed. As she grew older, however, she could not help but wonder why God gave children to those who didn't deserve them.

Her thoughts were interrupted by a loud male voice. "Excuse me, we need to get through."

It was the pallbearers; Sarah hadn't realized they were standing in their way. She watched as they lowered Aviela's body into the ground and felt a completely unexpected sense of relief flow into her spirit. Aviela was finally safe and at rest.

There were no sweet hymns sung as there might be at other burials, nor did the priest talk about the beautiful life that Aviela lived; the words, *"Ashes to ashes and dust to dust"* were required to hold all their grief. Still, there was something important about this gathering to pay their respects. As the priest concluded the ceremony by throwing a handful of dirt on Aviela's casket, the sudden noise fractured Sarah's reverie, and glancing across the grave she suddenly noticed Detective Askew standing somewhat stiffly behind Aviela's family.

Feeling unaccountably uncomfortable at his presence, Sarah averted her gaze and pretended not to notice him. She looked instead at Sandy, who was sitting in the front row, head down, nervously fidgeting with her wedding ring.

Aviela's parents had done most of the planning for the service. Sarah had offered to play a part in it, but they had not been receptive. Sarah tried not to take it personally, but she would have liked to honor the emerging young woman she had gotten to know over the past four months. It saddened her that the ceremony was devoid of the personal elements she would have included, perhaps reading some of the more hope-filled and self-reflective excerpts from Aviela's journal and inviting those who had known and cared about her—from whatever period of her life—a chance to speak.

But Sarah realized it was unhelpful to spend

too much time being angry with Aviela's parents; it wouldn't bring the girl back. Sarah knew they had loved their daughter in the way they thought was best and that their kicking her out when she was pregnant was perhaps done in the hopes that she would feel the harshness of the world and, like the biblical story of the prodigal son, return home, eager to obey their rules.

Sarah remembered that when she was young her own mother had occasionally resorted to what she termed "whippings" to get Sarah to behave. She'd told Sarah, "my parents taught me, 'spare the rod, spoil the child'," and although the whippings hadn't been particularly brutal, they were painful and humiliating, and Sarah had finally expressed to her mother that when she punished her in this way, it only made Sarah angry, and made her vow not to get caught the next time—it did nothing to address the source of the misbehavior, or to help her want to make better decisions next time.

Maybe Aviela's parents had decided jointly that they were not going to extend any help to Aviela when she got pregnant. *So many "maybes."*

When Sarah was growing up, it had seemed strange to her that Jesus loved children but that many religious people saw children as the property of adults. She would cringe when she heard a friend's mother tell her, "I brought you into this world and I can take you out!"

As she reflected on her upbringing, Sarah could feel anger building in her heart. She would ensure she kept that in mind when looking for an adoptive family for Aviela's child. Aviela's parents had already said they did not want the baby, and although Sarah could not laud their reasons for making this choice, she was relieved that they would not be bringing up a child in the narrow-minded and judgmental environment in which Aviela had so suffered.

And that was just it. Sarah knew Aviela's parents were merely responding to their own up-bringing. Sarah could feel compassion for them in this—surely they had not wanted their daughter murdered, and yet it had happened, and they would live with this fact for the rest of their lives.

In that moment, Sarah was struck by the degree to which parents re-inflict their own childhood pain upon their children. She made a mental note to lobby for the DFCS office to provide more information and support to families around the effects of trauma and how to begin to truly heal from it, rather than simply passing it from generation to generation.

With respect to Aviela's son, since there was no father on record who might be available to take the baby, the police had placed the infant with the Georgia Adoption Agency. Sarah and Kyle had talked about taking him themselves, but as much as they wanted to continue this connection with Aviela, they knew that they were not ready to parent a newborn.

As the burial came to a close Sarah took one last glance at the local paper's obituary she carried with her and shook her head.

At least the parents could have allowed Sarah to write something positive about Aviela in the funeral program. All they had included was a picture of her, the name of the pallbearers and a white dove on the back. If she had been allowed to write a little biography about Aviela, Sarah would have said that Aviela was a smart, considerate and sometimes playful kid who dreamed of becoming a scientist who would cure the world of cancer. She had a smile that could light up a room.

Sarah had offered, but Aviela's father had insisted on a simple photo.

"Baby, you deserved better," Sarah whispered as she folded the obituary and placed it in her purse. Aviela was the first "client" with whom Sarah had established such a close bond; it was something her boss and co-workers warned her about, and strongly discouraged, but Sarah knew from her studies that people who've been in unhealthy relationships—or been subjected to trauma—often struggle to maintain healthy relationships. One of the most effective treatments for survivors of trauma, Dialectical Behavioral Therapy, explicitly teaches interpersonal skills,

and encourages clients to understand that things (and people) are rarely all good or all bad.

Sarah knew it was essential to establish relationships characterized by care, trust and appropriate boundaries, so that the young people she worked with could experience healthy attachment.

And Aviela *had* begun to trust Sarah. Toward the end, Sarah could confidently say that Aviela had found in her someone who, unlike other people who may have abandoned or taken advantage of her, would do her best to keep Aviela's needs at the forefront of their relationship.

The two could talk about many things, and Sarah would share enough of her own personal struggles to assure Aviela that she was a real person, while always remembering that her age, and her role in Aviela's life, required her to keep the younger person's needs front and center.

Despite their closeness, however, there were subjects the two had not discussed. Like two people afraid of opening the wounds of the past, they had never talked about being abused and they rarely discussed their parents. Although Sarah had originally tried to get Aviela to share the story of the father of her child, she had soon seen it was a subject that remained too painful for Aviela to talk about.

As soon as the burial was over, Kyle had to leave her to go back to the shop, and Sarah went straight to the park and sat on a bench.

There, in a kind of personal memorial tribute to Aviela, she began to recollect all of the beautiful moments she'd spent with her. It was interesting how death changed one's perspective; some things that had seemed important at the time did not seem so now, while other elements, such as Aviela's wry sense of humor and the incredible strength Sarah knew it took for Aviela to open herself up to the possibility of trusting Sarah, were heartbreaking to consider.

Finally, Sarah knew she needed to move, and she walked back to the car, though she wasn't even sure where she would go. There didn't seem anything important enough to extract her from the pain she was feeling.

As Sarah drove out of the parking lot, desperately longing for the hands of the clock to rewind, she began to wish she had pushed harder to get Aviela to share the identity of her baby's father. If she had, maybe Aviela would be alive. Sarah realized she was feeling increasingly sure that the father of Aviela's child had something to do with her death. Who was he and why was he so hard to find?

CHAPTER FIFTEEN

SARAH LOOKED AT ALL THE school's trophies as she sat in the principal's office, waiting for the young man to show up. As she appreciated the trophy cabinet, she could not help but reflect that it had been years since she had been in a high school.

She recalled her last day of secondary school, when some of the boys—the jocks in particular— had taken the time to go around to the different classrooms, using spray paint to memorialize their names on the walls.

In contrast, Sarah and her group of friends had spent their time talking about how much they would miss each other and how they intended to keep in touch. None of the girls had intended to cry but when Hilda shed the first tear, Sarah followed and then they all huddled around each other for the last time. They made pinky promises—like little girls—to stay in touch with each other and then began to leave one by one.

It had been more than seven years since then, and the group had—sadly—long since stopped communicating with one another, except for the updates they posted on FaceBook, which was a poor substitute for in-person connection.

The school Sarah was visiting today wasn't just any ol' high school; it was Tucker High School, known for their great football team. The team had won two championships—one in 2017 and one in 2018—and the story of their wins was considered a kind of legend within the state. According to a sensationalist national newspaper that ran a story on the unique turnaround of Tucker High School, the school team had started the 2017 season at the bottom. For three straight games, they were known as a group of losers who were walloped by every other team. Team morale was so low that many of the best players left and parents constantly criticized the coach. Then, from nowhere, the coach began to marshal his troops to play the most interesting football games ever; now, the team was attracting the attention of national recruiters, and parents were even moving into the district in order to give their sons a chance to play on this team.

Sarah was there to speak with one of the players, Gerald, whom she believed could be a vital piece in solving the puzzle of Aviela's death. After getting Gerald's last name from Aviela's mother,

Sarah chose to interview him at the school. She knew that if she went to Gerald's house, she might not get much information because the young man might be unwilling to talk candidly in front of his parents, and Sarah needed all the information she could get.

She sat in the principal's air-conditioned office while the principal herself went to get Gerald from class. When the two entered the office, Sarah took in Gerald's clean-cut appearance, courteous hand-shake and cautious greeting. Sarah smiled and thanked the principal as she left the room, leaving them alone together to talk.

"Hi, Gerald. How are you doing?" Sarah asked as she motioned for the young man to take a seat.

"I'm ok, ma'am." The watchfulness in his eyes reminded Sarah that he had no idea who she was, nor why she had come to talk with him.

"I was Aviela's Advocate, and she mentioned that you guys had been together, and I wanted to come and ask you some questions."

"The police have asked me lots of questions. I don't know what happened to her, I haven't seen her for almost a year, and I didn't have anything to do with it."

Sarah realized belatedly that she should have started by letting Gerald know that she had no reason to suspect him of the murder; "Gerald, when Aviela talked to me about you, she had nothing but good things to say. She said you were a gentleman, and that she felt as though you actually cared for her as a person, in a way that no one else ever had."

Gerald relaxed perceptibly and nodded slightly.

"We was tight," he said, by way of agreement.

"Can you tell me a little bit about her, and your relationship?"

"We met in English class last year, and basically started hanging out together after school. She was really cool; she was smart, but she wasn't stuck up about it, like some girls. We were taking it slow, 'cuz she was younger, and plus, her dad hated my guts. He saw us together one day and got in my face, telling me he'd have me put in jail for dating his daughter. I told her we'd have to see each other on the down-low, but we didn't mind—it was almost like a game in a way. We'd see each other in English class, and pass notes, and we always sat together at lunch, and we'd post things on IG with captions that meant something to us, but her parents never guessed. And really Aviela's mom wasn't too against us dating—she just didn't want Aviela doing anything that would make her dad crazy.

But he went through her phone one day and saw a couple of selfies we'd taken together—even though it was nothing bad—Aviela's father beat her and told her that if we continued to see each other, he *would* find a way to stop us, and neither one of us wanted to take the risk."

Sarah was impressed with the way Gerald talked about their relationship, especially because he was so young.

"Were you guys having sex?" Sarah asked softly after a long pause.

Gerald glanced quickly away and then stole a look back at Sarah. His big brown eyes then fixed their gaze slightly above her head, as if he didn't want to make eye contact. She knew it was a kind of tactic he was using to gauge if she was worthy of any information he wanted to tell her.

"Well, ma'am... we liked each other a lot. But she wanted to go further than I did. I told her we had to wait until she was out of her dad's house. She didn't like that much."

Sarah leaned in to hear more as Gerald appeared ambivalent about their conversation. She noticed that his sentences would fade the longer he spoke. She reflected that he seemed unusually mature, and it was clear why Aviela might have fancied him; he didn't look as though he would have any problems with the ladies, with his handsome face and athlete's build. Still, Sarah felt that he didn't look like the type of boy she had thought the Aviela she knew would be attracted to.

Puzzled, Sarah asked, "So what made you such a gentleman to respect her age? Some boys would have jumped at the opportunity to have sex with a younger girl. I mean, you were seventeen. You're not that much older than she was."

Gerald seemed not to take offense at the question.

"Yes ma'am. But I had an experience I did not want to relive."

Gerald looked at Sarah as if he was trying to determine if he could trust her. He shifted his body's weight in the chair and looked toward the open blinds. Although the door was shut, he seemed to want to make sure no one would listen to what he was about to say.

"Well, when I was in ninth grade, I had a thing for my Global Studies teacher. She was tutoring me after school to help me get my grades up so I could join the junior varsity football team. Her schedule got busy and she offered to do the tutoring from her home so we FaceTimed.

One day she called me wearing only a lace tank top and running shorts and I thought she looked really good, and I told her. She asked me if I thought she was attractive, and when I said 'Yeah,' she said, 'Show me.'"

Sarah could clearly see that Gerald was conflicted about continuing. She could imagine where this might be heading, and she wasn't sure if she should stop him to remind him that she was a mandatory reporter, and that she would be required to report any incidents of abuse about which she knew. Sarah herself had ambivalent feelings about this reporting requirement, as she'd had numerous teens tell her that they'd learned never to tell anyone about the abuse they'd suffered because the state always stepped in, but with interventions that were invariably ineffective and often left the situation worse off than before. Sarah wasn't sure what the answer was, because clearly abusers needed to be stopped, but she wasn't convinced that taking the locus of control away from young people, especially older teens, was the best way to protect them from an abusive experience.

Anyway, before Sarah could say anything, Gerald continued, "For a minute I wasn't sure what she meant, and then it hit me, and I thought, 'Why not?' So I moved the camera so she could see for herself, and, well, yeah... things kind of went from there."

Sarah could feel herself turning red as an image of the described activities involuntarily intruded into her head. "Okay, I get the picture. Then what happened?"

Gerald continued on, as if having told this much, he might as well finish the story.

"Well, ma'am, we started fooling around and I started bragging to some friends and they went and told. The teacher got fired and went to jail. I still feel bad about what happened."

"Man," Sarah said heavily. "I can see why this experience taught you sex can be serious, and I'm sorry you had to go through that. On all levels. And I hope you know that this was not your fault; she was the adult, and regardless of whether you thought she was attractive or not she had the responsibility to *be* the adult and to think about what you needed and deserved from her, not what she might have wanted from you."

"Yeah, I know, and... well, I try to learn from everything that happens," Gerald said, looking up at her again, clearly back in the present and ready to be done talking about this part of his past.

"Was that why you told Aviela you guys should wait?" Sarah asked

"Yes, ma'am. I have several scholarship offers and I'm determined to make it out of here. I mean, come on! A black kid from the hood dating a white girl from the suburbs? You know all it would've taken was one 'credible' allegation and they would've thrown me in jail. We couldn't take that risk. We figured once she was done with high school she could come be with me wherever I ended up in school, and her parents wouldn't have any right to say anything. I mean, her dad would hate it, but that's on him."

"So what happened then? How come her dad kicked her out, if you guys had stopped seeing each other?" Sarah gently probed.

"I don't know. All I know is that she was here, and then suddenly she wasn't. They cut off her phone when she disappeared, so I had no way to find out."

"Do you have any idea who might have gotten her pregnant?"

"No ma'am; I hadn't even known she was

pregnant until I saw the news." It was clear that this both hurt and puzzled him. Then he asked abruptly, "And can you tell the police to stop coming around asking me to admit I'm the baby's father? I mean, I offered to give the detective DNA for a paternity test but he didn't want it. He said that if I gave him a written statement saying I was the father, he would close the case. That's bullshit," Gerald said angrily "they don't want to do their job and they want me to take the fall for it."

Then, as if he had just remembered something, he added, "Well, you may want to talk to the pastor of that big church in Decatur. You know, the one with the celebrity pastor. I heard she might have gone up there after her parents kicked her out, but I don't know if they know anything."

"Are you talking about Freedom United Baptist Church?" Sarah asked.

"Yes, that's the one. One of the girls Aviela used to hang with told me that after Aviela got kicked out, Aviela told her that the pastor would help find her a place to stay, and she said she saw Aviela getting into a black SUV after she made a phone call."

Sarah's lips came together to indicate that she was in deep thought.

"Hmmm, that's strange. Aviela never mentioned anything about this," Sarah murmured, almost to herself.

Then, looking at Gerald again she said,

"I appreciate your being willing to talk with me about this. I know that this must be very hard for you, and I want to tell you that I will do everything I can to find out what happened to Aviela; just know that she loved you and the emotional connection that you guys had."

Sarah got up and started to give him her hand, but impulsively she moved closer and gave him a hug. She wasn't sure it was the right thing to do and she felt awkward, but he said "thank you," and seemed vaguely comforted. They walked out of the office together, and Sarah thanked the principal, indicating with a tight smile that she would not be discussing their conversation with her.

As Sarah drove away, she said to herself, *looks like I will be going somewhere I haven't been in a while. Church!*

CHAPTER SIXTEEN

THE LARGE STEEPLE COULD BE seen from the highway miles away. It was a familiar landmark in the city and one that reflected Atlanta's unique history. Under the current pastor, Pastor Portland, the church had embarked on many charitable campaigns which saw the establishment of three soup kitchens for the homeless, and one location where people could donate clothing and those without could take whatever they needed.

Seeing the magnificent church, Sarah realized that it was even larger than she had imagined.

It was, without a doubt, the most beautiful building in the area. Some magnificent statues of Jesus were visible from afar, and she could see brightly colored murals on the outer walls of the church; Sarah wondered what stories they depicted. *Probably paintings of the last supper, or Jesus on the cross*, she thought. Those seemed the two most popular megachurch murals. Sarah had also seen Abraham's intended sacrifice of Isaac, and God's intervention depicted, and she wondered if God had tried to intervene in the case of Aviela. *Had God tried to use the pastor to forestall the death of the little one, or had God forsaken Aviela, just as the little dead girl had thought?*

The church was surrounded by strip malls, pawn shops, and a liquor store, none of which seemed out of place.

Sarah reflected that although she had perceived her current neighborhood to be quite depressing, seeing the church's surroundings, she recognized that she did not live in the worst part of Atlanta. As she surveyed the church lot she saw a few parked cars, around which lurked a few men who appeared, to Sarah's eye at least, rather menacing.

Sarah had heard that this church was one of the largest in Atlanta. Her mother had always wanted to visit, but her father was adamant that churches enslave people. When Sarah's mother protested this blanket condemnation, her father would bring up examples of religious fervor gone awry, such as the Atlanta bishop who had been accused of molesting several boys, and convinced most of his congregants he was innocent, as well as numerous examples of money siphoned off into decidedly worldly uses.

Sarah herself had mixed feelings about churches. Though they clearly provided many people with a much-needed sense of community, there were aspects of organized religion that seemed unhelpful at best, and potentially damaging at worst. In particular, she was inclined to find the whole concept of "sinning" problematic.

Many of the deeds religious leaders condemned as sins were in fact committed by hurt people looking for ways to cope; even if those behaviors weren't necessarily the healthiest, calling them sinful was a problem because instead of helping, it made people more prone to self judgement, which, ironically, only led to more self (and other) destructive behavior. If people understood their pain better they might alter their behavior; understanding seemed to Sarah to be a necessary precursor to changing one's actions.

Signs posted outside the church pointed Sarah toward the business office. She knew that Pastor Portland was a well-liked figure in the community. In fact, people had embraced him because he had turned his life of drugs and crime into one dedicated to serving God. Such miraculous stories of change were a huge catalyst for church growth, as many believed that the hand of the divine rested strongly on such people. Pastor Portland had parlayed his story of redemption into an appeal that made his one of the fastest-growing churches in the Southeast.

Knowing of the pastor's popularity, and imagining his busy schedule, Sarah had no idea if he would be in his office or not but she was hoping to speak with him about Aviela. Kyle had recommended that Sarah help Aviela by connecting her with his church services, and although Sarah had never taken him up on the suggestion, it was interesting that Gerald had said it was possible Aviela might have found her own way there before they'd even met.

As she passed through the doors, Sarah saw a number of people around Aviela's age mingling with older men and women who wore T-shirts printed with the church's name and image on the back, and STAFF on the front. There appeared to be some sort of celebration going on, as there was a table set up along one wall of the open room where several staff were handing out pieces of white and chocolate cake to the enthusiastic crowd of teens.

Sarah stopped outside the door labeled "Office," and since there was no one currently behind the desk, she paused to observe the kids, many of whom had tattoos of snakes, horned devils, and naked women visible on the arms, legs and shoulders not covered by their clothing. Some of the staff appeared to sport the same tattoos, suggesting that the pastor might have former gang members involved in helping save the younger generation.

Although there was a part of Sarah that felt distinctly out of place in this environment, a minority in the sense of having had such a comparatively privileged life, sheltered from the violence and trauma associated with the gangs, she made an effort to put genuine warmth into her smile as she nodded at or said hello to those who greeted her.

Sarah had printed out Aviela's photo in case the pastor did not already know who she was, though given the amount of media attention her killing had engendered, this seemed unlikely.

Now Sarah's the scent of the cake and lemonade from across the room, and her hungry stomach grumbled a little; she wished she felt comfortable enough to walk over and ask for a piece, but she knew this would not project the professional image she felt was necessary, so she contented herself with hoping her stomach would be quiet if she were actually granted an audience with the pastor.

"I'm sorry, is the pastor expecting you?" The 50-ish woman with deep mocha skin who now greeted Sarah had on a gorgeous shade of dark-red lipstick and a purple and gold scarf fluttered about her torso as she emerged from a room located behind the front office and looked at her inquiringly.

"No ma'am. My name is Sarah Clarkston. I'm from the Georgia Department of Family and Children's Services. I was hoping to catch him in the office to discuss the possibility of procuring services for our underserved youth."

Sarah had no intention of revealing the real

reason for her visit until she was actually meeting with the pastor in person. Sarah prayed that she conveyed the requisite level of authority, as the short, robust woman seated herself behind the desk and lowered her eyeglasses, looking up at Sarah and clearly appraising her with some doubt. After a long pause, she pointed toward the hallway saying, "Well, you're going to have to speak with someone from the youth department. They handle all our youth and young adults."

Deflated by the response, Sarah knew the woman meant business by her demeanor. Like Barbara, she looked like someone who would not mind putting Sarah in her place if she dared to pursue the matter any further. In fact, the woman had somewhat ostentatiously shifted her attention and begun typing.

Just as Sarah turned to leave, however, a short, thick man wearing a blue pin-stripe suit and red patterned tie walked through the door at the back of the office through which the woman had earlier appeared. Sarah was almost certain this was the pastor, and she felt herself tense involuntarily at the sight of him, but she knew she needed to appear composed if she were to succeed in maneuvering her way into a private meeting.

As he appeared to register her presence, she smiled widely and lifted her chin in greeting.

Turning toward his secretary, he said, "Hey Hattie, get my driver. Let him know I will be ready to go in about twenty minutes." His words, and the authoritative tone, confirmed Sarah's suspicion that he was indeed the pastor. She was not going to miss this opportunity seemingly presented to her from above, and before the secretary could answer, Sarah exclaimed confidently,

"Why hello, Pastor Portland!" She had learned the power of tonal manipulation from her socialite mother, who taught Sarah the importance of clear articulation coupled with a warm tone; her mother had been known for her lovely voice— and the ability to stop people in their tracks with a mere word or two. The pastor turned back toward Sarah and tilted his head. His eyes narrowed as he obviously scanned his memory to determine from where he might know her.

"Wait; aren't you Jacob Clarkson's daughter?"

Sarah wasn't surprised the pastor knew her father, but she was a bit taken aback that he would recognize her. She had obviously changed significantly in the twenty or so years since the pastor had been caught with some drugs and had needed her dad's help to get and keep him out of jail. He had been locked up for a second time some years later and faced the possibility of 25 to life if convicted for the third time. Sarah believed that it was the prospect of significant jail time that had precipitated the pastor's radical life change.

He flashed her a smile, which she pushed herself to return as she answered,

"Yes, pastor; that is indeed my father. And it has been a long time."

She saw the secretary's face tighten a bit but she did not care. Now that she held the pastor's full attention, she would not relinquish it. "I am sorry pastor, but do you think you could spare some time to talk?"

The pastor immediately extended his hand for a handshake, "Sure, come with me out front. I have a few minutes before my driver arrives and we can enjoy the afternoon sunshine."

He ushered Sarah outside, making a slight production of holding the heavy door for her while she passed through, while he asked why it was she had come to see him. As she told the pastor that she had heard many good things about the work the church was doing with young people, she saw a car approaching; Pastor Portland held up a finger and said, "Just a second, my driver is here already. I'll let him know I'll be a few minutes and then we can talk."

A black Lincoln Navigator pulled up in front of them, tinted window lowered, as the pastor strode briskly to the vehicle. Sarah, having settled herself for a brief wait while the pastor spoke with his driver, looked absently at the man driving the Navigator, and almost passed out. Her stomach churned as she recognized the driver as the very same man she had seen Aviela struggling to get away from that morning, so many months ago, behind her apartment building.

Sarah couldn't tell if he had recognized her, as he wore dark shades in the midday sun and his head was turned toward the pastor, who re-joined Sarah almost immediately as the Naviga-tor pulled off into a corner of the wide parking lot.

"Sorry for the interruption," he said, "you were saying...?"

But Sarah was so shaken by this unexpected twist that she found herself stammering inanely "Oh, yes, I was saying that I know that the church has done so much good work with young people, and... I know you're busy and maybe we could schedule another time to talk more about it?"

She knew she sounded odd, but the confir-mation of the link between Aviela and the people who surrounded this man warned her that her worst fears might well be founded, and until she had a better understanding of what exactly might be going on she decided that discretion might be the better part of valor.

———

Determined to find another way to get the an-swers she needed, Sarah walked into the police station later that afternoon, one day before her scheduled appointment with Detective Askew.

"Hello Miss Sarah. I'm surprised to see you here today," Detective Askew said as he looked up from his desk to face her.

He was telling the truth; Sarah had had the distinct feeling she was being left out of the loop on Aviela's case, and she had not been willing to wait. Given Clifford Askew's reputation in his department, Sarah believed that he knew more than he was telling her—hence her decision to catch him off-guard by showing up early.

"I'm sorry to surprise you, detective," she said, a bit disingenuously, "but some things have come up and I just had to meet with you."

Detective Askew waved it off with an air of little concern. "No worries, Sarah. Please have a seat." As Sarah lowered herself into the chair facing his desk, he rose. "Coffee?"

"Yes, please."

"I'll be right back. Stay right there," the detective said as he disappeared from the office.

Sarah reclined further into the chair and was immediately appreciative of the office's comfortable furnishings. As she mulled over the comforts of the detective's office, she saw a file labelled **"Free Soles"** in bold green capital letters. Even though she knew that it was not unusual for the group to send files to detectives who worked with them, something in her nudged her to take a quick look at its content. Peering around furtively and seeing no one, she brought the folder closer. As she studied its contents, her eyes widened.

Quickly finishing the document, she dropped the paper back into the folder and slid the folder back where it had been, pondering its content as she waited.

Lost in thought, she looked at the wall of the office and could not help admiring the seemingly extraordinary feats which the detective had performed over the years for the city.

Sarah got up in order to look more closely at one picture—dated June 21st, 2002—in which she saw a smiling mayor pin a badge on the uniform of Officer Askew, who, at that point, had yet to become a detective. She remembered that case vividly, because Barbara still mentioned it in passing to the unit.

The case had involved the daughter of a high-profile politician who had been kidnapped by a group of men as she walked home from school. In a period where there were few closed-circuit TV cameras documenting street activity, Officer Askew had managed to piece together fragments of information from numerous sources to identify the girl's kidnappers.

He had discovered the unthinkable—the politician's wife, and *mother of the child*, had been the brains behind the kidnapping—because of her desire to help her husband get into the spotlight for the upcoming elections.

Sarah surveyed the array of other pictures

on Detective Askew's wall and marveled at some of the details. One showed the detective playing with kids at a local school after educating them on security measures. Another showed a younger Askew smiling into the camera while holding the hanger of a parachute, suggesting a fondness for skydiving.

One framed picture showed the detective paying rapt attention to something being said by the governor of the state. The fifth picture showed a little girl with curly hair and the cutest eyes in the world. This photo seemed new and Sarah paused to have a closer look. As she wondered whether the girl was Askew's daughter, her thoughts were truncated by the detective's return.

"Wondering who the pretty angel is?" he asked with a beaming smile. "Her name's Tori; she's my little goddaughter."

Sweat began to form under Sarah's armpits. She hoped her nervous movements would not give her away as she took the coffee with a smile and sat down.

"So, what's up? What would you like to know?" The detective asked.

It took her a full minute before Sarah found her voice and began to speak, "I would like to know if any information about the..."

The ring of an incoming call from Detective Askew's phone stopped her in her tracks. With an upraised hand, the detective signaled to Sarah to wait while he took the call.

"Hey, what's good? Hunh! Why would he want that? Alright, meet me at that restaurant in ten."

Sarah knew from the decisive sound of his voice that the detective had already dismissed her; whoever had been on the phone obviously took precedence, and, again, she would have to wait to get any satisfaction. Indeed, his next words confirmed her premonition;

"Miss Sarah, I'm afraid we have to postpone this conversation. An emergency has just arisen to which I need to attend immediately."

Damn, Sarah thought as she stood and offered thanks for the coffee and his time. She felt she had been thwarted again by unseen hands preventing her from weaving together the threads of the mystery of what had happened to Aviela. From the paper in the file, she had gotten a vital piece of the puzzle, but she needed Detective Askew to verify the information before she drew any conclusions.

She heard Detective Askew say, "I hope we can meet up later to finish this conversation," as he closed the door behind them.

Then, he escorted her to her car and went on his way.

CHAPTER SEVENTEEN

A s she sat behind the steering wheel of her car, Sarah's mind churned over the disparate pieces of the puzzle like a raging sea. So many half-answered questions lay before her, the most critical of which remained: *who was Aviela's killer?*

Who was Aviela's baby daddy? Was it fear— or something else—that had kept her from talking about him? What was Aviela's real intent when she ran away from Free Soles?

Some of Sarah's colleagues had suggested that Aviela had run off to return to the life of the streets, but Sarah was almost certain this was not the case. But without answers to these questions, there might not ever be a way to know for sure.

"Damn, why does this have to be so complicated?" Sarah muttered as she started her car and began to drive. It was getting late and she had no destination in mind; no intention of going to her office to do paperwork after hours, even though she was sure it was piling up as she was running around trying to solve a murder. She had half a mind to visit Aviela's mother as she had promised, but feared that might upset the woman without being likely to lead to any more useful information.

Almost on autopilot, Sarah found herself driving to the place where she could feel Aviela's aura most intensely.

Her gravesite.

———

Sarah parked her car near the graveyard office. The last time she had visited Aviela her car had had trouble making it up the hill to her grave. Today, although the light was already starting to fade from the sky, she decided to use the stone steps. She exited her car and began climbing. Halfway up she stopped to catch her breath. *This is great,* she thought, only half-joking, *I get a workout while clearing my mind.*

As she approached the gravesite, she noticed there were no fresh bouquets on the plain concrete headstone and she felt the intense sadness wash over her again, along with an anger that Aviela's baby daddy refused to acknowledge her, even in death.

As she was considering all that had happened, she saw two vehicles enter the graveyard. From her vantage point on top of the hill, she could not make out their drivers, but even in the dim light, both cars looked familiar. One was a black sport utility vehicle and the other one looked like an unmarked police car. As they drove up the hill, Sarah thought the second car looked like a black Lincoln Navigator. *That's Pastor Portland's car,* she thought, *but who is that in the car in front of him?* Sarah immediately thought of dashing back to her car but realized they would see her running. Her feet felt heavy. "Shit, think, think!" she whispered to herself.

As she looked wildly around for cover, she noticed a couple of larger gravestones slightly beyond Aviela's. Sarah quickly darted behind the one to the left. Silently giving thanks for her diminutive size, she crouched and pressed herself flat against the stone to fit within its shadow. Now she would only be visible if they walked past Aviela's grave. She tried to slow her breathing, but her mind raced as she considered whether they would see her car, parked in the shade of a tree near the business office. It was not exactly in plain view, due to the bushes that flanked the small parking lot, but Sarah was fairly certain that the pastor's driver would recognize it as hers if he got a good look at it. *I just have to hope they're too focused on whatever it is they're doing here,* she thought to herself.

Although from her hiding spot she could no longer see the men, Sarah could hear the sounds of two car doors closing in quick succession. The crunch of gravel under what might be two sets of feet moved in her direction. The sun's rays pierced the dark clouds as the noises stopped just a few feet from Aviela's headstone. She could hear labored breathing and wondered from whom it was coming.

Then a person spoke, and although Sarah was not totally surprised, she was still frightened as she recognized the voice as that of her father's old friend, Detective Askew.

"Hey look; calm down. You're..."

Another male voice, less recognizable but still familiar, sounded both angry and shrill,

"Don't you tell me to calm down! You assured me you had this under control, and why in the hell would you have me meet you at her gravesite?"

Detective Askew's mocking tone carried perfectly through the still air; "Just a little reminder of what's at stake here, buddy. On the phone, you said you were going to stop the payments and let things cool off. I want to remind you we are standing over the gravesite of the murdered mother of your child."

As the puzzle pieces clicked into place in Sarah's mind, she stifled a gasp.

Detective Askew continued, "You stop those payments and I *will* make sure the result of the DNA test I ordered makes its way over to our homicide division."

The other man's response provided the final bit of evidence assuring Sarah that she had been right about the SUV being Pastor Portland's as he said: "I can't believe I let myself get involved with this mess. You said if I opened up that group home for teens as a cover for your operation, you would keep me out of this."

He continued, "I should've just gone to jail the night you busted me with that 'ho and cut my losses."

Detective Askew raised his voice; "No one told you to fuck the girls and get them pregnant; we were in this for the money, not for entertainment. If you had kept your dick in your pants we wouldn't be having this talk. That was what got your ass in this mess."

From the sound of his voice, it appeared Pastor Portland was beginning to comprehend the magnitude of the trouble he was in. "My driver recognized Sarah when she came snooping around the church the other day. I brushed her off before she could start asking questions. He recognized her as the same woman who saw him roughing up Aviela behind her apartment building."

"Yeah, I know. She came around my office today," Detective Askew responded.

"What? Does she know?" The pastor sounded both shocked and scared.

"Nope, she does not know 'cuz I left the office."

"I can assure you she knows nothing. I didn't even know she was snooping around. I closed the case and made the notes look as though we thought it might have been the work of a transient. I guess I will have to pay her father a visit to see if he can talk some sense into her."

Pastor Portland immediately asked "Why would you drag him into this? I was a client of his long ago. I don't need him snooping around too. Shit. Seems like his criminal seeking gene has been passed down to that daughter of his."

Detective Askew's voice was slightly amused as he reassured him, "Oh, don't worry. The attorney and I are old friends. Plus, we have some unfinished business."

As the men could be heard crunching their way back to their respective cars, Sarah heard Detective Askew say to the pastor,

"And, man, if you hadn't had your damn driver kill her, we would have been okay. She wasn't about to say anything, but you got impatient."

She did not hear the pastor's response as his voice was drowned out by the sound of the car's engine starting.

Sarah waited a long time after she was sure the cars had both left before slowly emerging from her hiding place. Her legs were cramped, and as she hobbled down the stone steps in the dark, her mind was swirling.

CHAPTER EIGHTEEN

T HE SUDDEN POUNDING ON HIS door jolted him
awake. Sal was barking wildly, and, startled,
Kyle rolled over, briefly tangled in the covers, before reaching into his bedside table drawer and
grabbing his silver Smith and Wesson .45 handgun. Although he considered himself someone
who tried to look for the good in all people, there
was no denying that there had been increasing
amounts of anti-gay and anti-immigrant violence
lately, and Kyle had no intention of becoming
a victim. He knew the statistics that personal
handguns were more likely to injure the gun
owner or a family member, whether by acci-
dent or domestic violence or a suicide attempt,
but Kyle didn't have a partner and he knew he
himself would be careful. He'd taken the recommended training course, and he felt confident
that he would be able to use the weapon for its
intended purpose. Now, heading to the door to
see who was pounding on it so loudly, he picked

up his phone to check the time and was shocked to see nine missed calls from Sarah.

He would call her back as soon as he dealt with whoever was banging on his door; he paused to put on a pair of jeans, and then he heard, "Open the door, Kyle. It's me, Sarah."

"Sarah?" he managed to say as he dropped his phone and quickly returned his gun to its place in the nightstand drawer.

Sarah continued to knock on the door, more softly now as she could hear Sal's long nails on the entry floors, and Kyle's voice coming toward the door. She heard the lock being unbolted and finally the door opened. She saw the "Hey-it's-too-early-for this-kind-of-shit" look that Kyle gave her and whispered her apologies.

"But," she said, "I really need to talk to you."

Kyle's irritation disappeared and he pulled her into the apartment and wrapped his arms around her as Sal tried to jump up on her and Kyle firmly ordered him to stop.

"What is it baby? Come in! You look like you're freezing." He was right. She was chilled. However, it was predominantly fear that was making her insides feel frozen.

Kyle led her through the hall and into the living room, saying, "Have a seat. I'll get you something to drink." Sal came immediately and sat on Sarah's feet, leaning into her and panting heavily from the excitement of her unexpected arrival, while Kyle went into his kitchen, reached into his cabinet and retrieved a glass.

Then he wondered if coffee would be better, given how cold she was. He could make it later, though, after she told him why she had come; water would be enough to help her regain her equanimity. When he placed the glass on the table in front of her, Sarah jumped at the noise. Kyle found that an odd reaction and tried to imagine what was going on with his friend, who was clearly in the grip of strong emotion.

He sat on the leather couch next to Sarah— on the side not already occupied by Sal's solid self—close enough to let the heat from his body both warm and comfort her while he grabbed the plush throw lying across the back of the couch and wrapped it around her, rubbing one hand over her back, where he could feel her heart thumping.

"Oh my God, you are shaking. And this is not just from cold. What is it?"

It was hard for Sarah to sit still, and she didn't seem ready to talk; she was just sitting. Kyle got back up and said, "You're going to need a little more than a glass of water. Wait a minute."

In the kitchen, he splashed some Crown Royal and Coke into a glass, added a single ice cube and brought it back into the living room. As he handed her the drink, he heard Sarah whisper,

"They, they..."

Kyle moved closer and again wrapped his

arms around her. Then, he reached out and grabbed the drink, which was shaking nervously in her hand.

"Okay. Try to slow down and tell me what happened," he said as he helped steady her hand, eventually taking the glass back again and placing it on the coffee table. He saw that it was difficult for her to talk and decided that she should speak at her own pace.

The reply came in between whimpers, "They killed her, Kyle."

"Who?"

"Detective Askew and Pastor Portland. I... I saw them..." Sarah's words became incoherent at that point, leaving Kyle totally lost. He offered her a reassuring hand squeeze and asked, "What? You're scaring me, honey. What happened?"

Sarah paused and stared at Kyle. Then, as if she couldn't bear sitting any longer, she threw the blanket off and rose to her feet, knocking over her water glass but apparently totally unaware of the liquid spreading across the patterned rug. "You told me I should take Aviela to him!" she said angrily, and Sal whimpered, looking from one to the other as if unsure how to help.

It was too much information to process; Kyle could only stare at her. "Sarah, what are you talking about? You're not making any sense."

Placing her hand on her chest and fighting to catch her breath, Sarah grabbed her purse.

Then she maneuvered around Sal and the coffee table and began to back toward the front door. "Pastor Portland. He had Aviela killed."

Kyle knew he had to be careful at that moment as Sarah was clearly not in her rational mind. Without knowing what she had seen, he had no way of knowing if what she was saying was accurate, but there was no doubt as to the intensity of her emotion, and he knew that if he tried to move closer, she might react violently, so he remained sitting and simply entreated,

"Sarah, please tell me what happened. And of course you can stay here if you're in danger."

Sarah stopped moving and squinted at him, obviously trying to ground herself and remembering why she had come to him in the first place.

"No, I don't want to put you in any danger, but I do need your help figuring out what to do," Sarah said as she sat down again.

She managed to recount the story of what she had heard in the cemetery, including the fact that they knew she was poking around, and by the time she had finished, Kyle looked at her seriously and said,

"Your place is the first place they will look for you, honey. You can't go back there. You need to be someplace safe until we can make sure we can find a way to get them where they won't be able to get you first. I know you don't want to, but you gotta go home to your parents."

Sarah groaned as if he had punched her in the stomach. "No, Kyle. I can't go there. I just can't."

But Kyle would have none of it. He helped her to her feet, collected his car keys and told her they could stop at a store to grab anything she thought she would need, but he was taking her to her parents' and that was final.

CHAPTER NINETEEN

T HE OFFICE WAS QUIET. REFLECTED light from the city skyline helped to softly illuminate Jacob's corner office. A light clicking sound of fingers tapping on keyboard keys interrupted the silence. He sat at his desk, laptop perched on the edge of it, working after-hours.

His firm no longer required the insane weeks Jacob had invested as a young attorney starting out in the public defender's office, or when he finally struck out on his own almost two years ago. Now, he had hired and shaped the talent who could, for the most part, keep things running smoothly while he maintained a presence, brought in new business and sorted out the occasional office issue.

The acceptance that he would be at work long into the evening, however, kept his wife of more than twenty years from expecting him at home, and this was the time of day he loved best, when he felt most professionally alive, and his legal creative juices flowed.

As a form of compensation for the time spent away from home, he'd always made sure that Rachel's material needs were met. She got the money to buy jewelry for social events, for spa visits and country club dues where she met with other women with more money than things to do with it. And, although Jacob didn't know it, some of that money was being directed toward a couple of charities Rachel had decided were worthy.

Jacob thought about Rachel now as he worked on a major civil case assisting a woman who was suing her doctor for sexual assault. The woman had been referred to a detox center to get help for alcohol abuse.

Rather than providing help, however, the doctor, a distinguished-looking white man with a shock of silver hair, administered the date rape drug Rohypnol, and raped her while she was under its influence. Cases like this repulsed Jacob. On a general scale of crimes, sex crimes ranked as the most despicable for him, which was part of the reason he enjoyed taking on pro bono cases that brought some sort of recompense to the survivors of sexual crimes.

As he continued to look at the police report detailing the doctor's confession, he shook his head disdainfully, *What kind of idiot would throw his life away like that?!*

As soon as the thought formed in his head, however, Jacob wanted to retract it. It felt too much like a case of a blind man accusing another blind man of not seeing. When he was young, his mama had told him that everyone inevitably does stupid shit, and he ought to make sure that his personal record was unblemished before throwing stones at others. He sighed, wishing he had not tempted fate by uttering those condemnatory words. Jacob knew he was in no position to talk; though his own transgression was not sexual in nature, he, too, had built his house upon a rocky foundation.

Jacob Googled the doctor's name. What he noticed first were the articles that concerned the crime the doctor was accused of committing, but it was interesting to Jacob to see the number of links to articles the doctor had written and published in reputable medical journals. The doctor was also the subject of an article, dated eight months back, referencing a charity event in Philadelphia to benefit sick children, where the doctor had donated $75,000.

"Damn." Jacob whispered as he saw a smiling picture of the doctor and his family, which consisted of a wife, two sons and a daughter. Jacob knew that whatever came out of the trial, the doctor's family, and his life, would not emerge unscathed.

Suddenly, his office door swung open, causing him to flinch. Jacob relaxed when he saw it was just Abraham, the janitor. Abraham flushed when he saw the boss clicking away at the system and immediately made to leave, but Jacob's voice caught him, "No, come on in Abraham. I was just packing up to go home."

"You sure sir? I can come back and clean your office last." Abraham returned, his hand still on the door. He did not wish to bother Jacob when he was working. "Yes, I'm sure." Jacob responded as he grabbed his client's file and began to place it in his briefcase. He looked at Abraham and found himself wanting to ask him a question.

The janitor was bent over, unwinding the cord to the vacuum cleaner. Then, in a routine that he had performed hundreds of times, Abraham moved to the wall to insert the plug. The vacuum cleaner looked like a toy in his hand. Anyone who came in at that moment would notice that he was a tall, intimidating-looking figure.

A black male in his mid-forties, people sometimes thought Abraham looked more like a bodyguard than a janitor. It was not uncommon to see ladies flirt with him even during office time, and he could not resist flexing his arms whenever he could. However, Jacob liked the man and had given him the cleaning contract to his office two years prior.

Abraham now looked up and noticed that Jacob was watching him intently. He paused and removed his earbuds with an inquiring look. He loved listening to R&B and its queen, Beyoncé, which seemed to be a queer combination at times. "I'm sorry sir. What is it, am I disturbing you?"

Jacob laughed and waved his hand again, signaling for Abraham to relax. Then, his face adopted a serious look as he continued, "Abraham. Quick question, have you ever done something you regretted?

"I wouldn't be human if I hadn't, sir." Jacob replied swiftly.

"You're a hard-working man. You couldn't possibly have done anything that bad." Jacob said with some curiosity, as he moved back to his chair and settled himself, looking attentively at Abraham as he did so. He realized he really wanted to know what Abraham's past contained.

Apprehension registered on Abraham's face as he sensed that the conversation was going somewhere he might not want it to. Slowly, he removed his gloves and placed them in his back pocket. "Sir, is this a personal or a business conversation?"

"Relax. You have been working for me for a couple of years, I really value your work and I know nothing about you. I mean, what's the worst thing you've done? Drop out of high school and couldn't land a decent job?" Jacob asked in his most reassuring voice, which he hoped would ease the janitor's fears.

Abraham's wry smile indicated he found Jacob's assessment of him amusing.

"No, sir. I owned a business."

Smiling in puzzlement now, Jacob asked the other man for clarification;

"I don't understand, how was that bad?" He was not sure where the conversation would lead, but it only now struck him that even though he and Abraham were nearly of the same age, he had not given Abraham's past life much thought.

"Yes, sir, APS LLC."

Jacob moved from his chair to sit on the edge of his desk and folded his arms, a sign that invited Abraham to tell him more.

Abraham nodded, and for a moment silence reigned. Then, Jacob said, "So, what happened?"

"Well, I guess what happened is I did some stupid things."

"Like what?"

Abraham put down the vacuum cleaner and removed a handkerchief from his pocket to wipe his face. "I hope this won't cost me my job?" he asked with a look of concern. His expression indicated that he would rather not speak about the incident at all. Nevertheless, he realized that he had stirred Jacob's interest.

"No. This is off the record." Jacob answered.

"Boy, I have heard that one before," Abraham said with a half-smile. Then, he delved into his story.

"Ten years ago, I had a beautiful family. I was

married to an angel and had two children. We lived in a nice five-bedroom, two-story brick home in Stone Mountain. I worked as a club promoter. I was making big money too, man. I booked all the big acts. Kid Rock, Eminem, Snoop Dog, Ice Cube, Puff Daddy, Biggie Smalls."

Jacob leaned forward with his mouth open. "Man, BIGGIE SMALLS?!" He slammed his hand on the desk and leaned back, "Man that must have been amazing!"

Abraham continued, "Yes, I was once invited to a private party at Dr. Dre's house and I caught the bug. I saw the big house, fancy cars, and all the pretty women and all of a sudden I was displeased with my own life." Abraham pointed at a chair in front of Jacob's desk and murmured, "May I?"

"Sure, go ahead, have a seat."

"You see, I haven't talked about this in years. Took a while to put it all behind me," Abraham continued as he inhaled deeply. "I started hanging out with those guys a lot more and before I knew it, I was involved in illegal activity. I served five years in prison for money laundering."

Jacob saw that Abraham was beginning to feel more uncomfortable, "Hey: if you don't want to talk about this, I understand."

"No, to be honest with you, it's kinda therapeutic talking about it. Part of my probation was going to local high schools and speaking to youth about the dangers of the fast life." Abraham replied as his face betrayed a hint of pride.

"If you don't mind my asking, what happened to your family?"

"My wife left me. But I don't blame her." Abraham said, matter-of-factly. It looked as if he had come to accept the loss as an inevitability and had moved on from grieving over it.

"She allows me to see the kids and I'm grateful for that. But I would give anything to have my family back." Then, Abraham seemed to stop focusing on himself and faced Jacob. "Sir, sorry for rambling. What about you? Any regrets?"

Jacob seemed not to be taken aback by the sudden turn in the conversation, but he knew that, given his position, he wasn't about to reciprocate with the same level of candor. "I guess so. But hey, like you said, we wouldn't be human if we didn't all have something we regret."

"You've got that right, sir." Jacob smiled at the umpteenth time that Abraham called him "sir," "You don't have to call me sir. Call me Jacob."

The man simply smiled and seemed to mentally decide against calling his boss by his name. Then, he began to stand, "well, I guess I better get back to cleaning. The kids like to Face-Time me before they go to bed. Want to make sure I'm where I'm supposed to be," he said with a smile.

"Tell you what Abraham. Take the rest of the evening off."

Abraham's eyes widened in surprise, "You sure sir...? I mean Jacob?"

"Sure. See you tomorrow." With that, Jacob closed his laptop and picked up the phone to call Rachel.

CHAPTER TWENTY

S HE WAS BACK HOME, BUT the decision was not what she might have made if she'd had limitless options. Sarah looked around the house and memories of her past washed over her. The good memories came first—like the time her mother came back from a safari in Zimbabwe with a hand-carved wooden zebra for her; the zebra was still here, he sat on the table in the entryway, next to a carved wooden bowl that held keys and mail.

Also, there, on the wall of the dining room, was a matted and framed painting she'd done in 3rd grade. Sarah vividly recalled the look on her father's face when he saw it, and the sound of his voice telling her he was proud of her. It was unusual for Jacob to give any form of commendation, and although Sarah now knew that this reticence was likely the result of his own upbringing, he was not the kind of parent who found it easy to tell Sarah "good job," and she'd often wished that he were not so hard to please.

On that particular day, however, he had taken one look at the picture and beamed broadly. The painting reflected a tiger in stride, the colors brightly splashed across the entire canvas, and when she had told her father that the tiger depicted him, he might even have teared up. At any rate, Sarah remembered well the unaccustomed sense of pleasure in his praise.

Now, as she walked into her bedroom, she stopped in her tracks. Her Usher and Justin Timberlake posters were still on the wall. Sarah and her friends growing up had all fawned over the two superstars. She chuckled at the realization that it felt a little as though her parents were expecting her to move home at some point. Sarah knew, however, that there was no way she would prolong her stay beyond what was necessary. She regarded this period as a time and place to remain safe until she could determine what to do with the information she had discovered about Aviela's death.

The queen-size bed was still made up with the light blue comforter and yellow oversized pillows Sarah had chosen in opposition to her mother's wishes. When decorating the nursery in their first house in anticipation of Sarah's arrival, Rachel had gone to town, covering every surface with some variation of the color pink, and though Sarah had long-since made it clear that she would rather have almost any color other than pink, Rachel had had a hard time letting Sarah pick her own colors for the new room, though eventually, and ungraciously, she had acquiesced. Rachel hated the fact that her little girl did not share her own love of pink. Even when her friends pointed out that the color pink could be seen as representing a problematic tendency to equate femininity with weakness, Rachel had not given a damn and responded by buying her daughter yet another pink dress.

Sarah reflected that a lot had changed since her mother had been a girl, both in terms of style and substance, and that at least some of the conflicts they'd had might be attributable to this difference in the cultures in which they'd each grown up, and the ways in which their environments had shaped their expectations of what was possible.

Sarah had waited until the first light came before calling her mom from Kyle's apartment and asking if she could come home for a few days. Her mom had said "yes, of course," without asking why. However, Sarah knew her mother well enough to be sure that Rachel would not allow the question of why her daughter had suddenly decided to move back home, however briefly, slide by.

She knew that the conversation would come sooner or later. However, she was not prepared just yet to reveal the details. Sarah's reminiscing was interrupted by her mom calling for her to come downstairs for dinner.

"Honey, come down. Dinner is almost ready." The irresistible smell of Rachel's Curried Chicken, potatoes, rice and peas, and cornbread filled the air. Despite Sarah's suspicion that cooking was a skill so linked to women's traditional household roles that to be proud of it was almost anti-feminist, she knew her mom gained great satisfaction from her culinary skills, and Sarah was certainly not able to resist the siren call of the thought of that delicious food. She now hurried in the direction of the back staircase which led directly down to the kitchen, but her pace slowed as she walked past her dad's office.

This was a room she'd frequented as a child whenever Jacob was around. She peeked into the room now and noticed that his desk was crowded with photos of the two of them together. *Those were the fun times,* she thought, as she exhaled deeply. Tears welled up in her eyes.

Memories of falling asleep in her father's office and him picking her up and carrying her to bed made her smile. Those were the periods when she had seen him as a fearless tiger who would do anything to ensure her safety.

He had chosen to use the room next to hers as his office so he could be close to her when she was a little girl. Of course, this had become annoying when she was a teenager because it was hard to talk on the phone or have fun on social media with her dad next door.

"Sarah." Her mother yelled again. This time, her voice indicated she was walking toward the stairs to reiterate her dinner summons.

"Mom, I'm coming."

As Sarah entered the kitchen, she immediately went to the stove and lifted the lids off the pots one by one. The sight was both familiar and enticing. It had been normal for her mom to cook as if she was preparing a buffet, but Sarah saw that her mother had improved her tendency to cook for a crowd considerably. "Mom, I sure do miss your cooking."

"Well sweetie, you know you're always welcome back home," Rachel said as she playfully slapped Sarah's hands off the pots. It was a routine mother and daughter loved to engage in, and one that always bonded them together.

"Thanks Mom. Is Dad joining us for dinner?"

Rachel rolled her eyes and exhaled, "I sure hope so. He will be so glad you're home." She had a look of optimism on her face that Sarah did not wish to squash with a negative response.

"I'm just visiting, Mom," she managed finally, hoping her response didn't sound overly rejecting.

"That's all I meant honey."

Sarah studied Rachel and realized with some surprise that her mother was sober.

Rachel had not told Sarah that she had begun

seeing a counselor recently, and had cut back on her drinking significantly, a decision that had brought her and Jacob closer. He had begun coming home from work much earlier recently and the two went out for dinner once a week.

Rachel knew that although it might be tempting to blame the lack of intimacy in her marriage on Jacob's workaholism, things were never all one sided; things would have been better if she had started reducing her alcohol intake earlier, but she was happy that their relationship was improving. Jacob had been so delighted with Rachel's diminished drinking that he had planned a vacation in August for them in Bermuda.

As Sarah observed her mother, she could tell that the older woman was in a happier state of mind that was not induced by alcohol. Rachel's brown skin was glowing and she was smiling. Sarah didn't want to dim the mood by telling her about her problems so she remained silent regarding everything related to Aviela.

Rachel's cell phone, lying on the kitchen table next to Sarah, rang, startling Sarah so much that she jumped to her feet so fast the chair tipped over behind her. Concerned, Rachel rushed over, looking her daughter full in the face with a serious expression, "Baby are you okay? Why are you so jumpy?"

"It's okay Mom. It's nothing," Sarah said, as her mother helped her pick up the chair. Rachel still held the phone whose ring had precipitated the commotion, and she now spoke into it; "Hello... oh, okay baby. See you soon."

"It's just your father letting me know he's on his way home." Rachel continued to observe her daughter with a furrowed brow as Sarah sat herself back down at the table.

Then, deciding that she needed to share the real reason she had returned to her parents' house, Sarah said, "Mom, I need to tell you why I came home."

Rachel walked over to the stove and began to warm the food. "Child, I know. I was just waiting for you to be ready to tell me what's going on. You forget I gave birth to you and raised you. I know how you are. Just too stubborn to admit when you need help." She returned to her seat and gazed reassuringly into Sarah's face.

Sarah frowned, as she knew that Rachel had this part of her personality pegged correctly. When she was growing up, she hadn't exactly been the poster child for meekness, yet she had often found it difficult to confide in her parents. Being vulnerable didn't feel comfortable when she knew how much her parents already worried about her, and how they would leap to try to help her find a solution, when sometimes, all she wanted was someone who could hear her. When they asked if she was okay, she would just shrug and say, "everything's cool," and then go to her room.

Sarah cleared her throat and began to talk,

"Mom, I let a girl from my job down. She trusted me and now she's DEAD!"

Her voice, which had begun almost inaudibly, had reached a point where it was exceptionally high. She could not bear to look her mother in the eyes and placed her head on her arms which rested on the table.

Rachel walked up behind her and stroked Sarah's back with her hand for a moment, then she pulled up a chair and sat next to Sarah, who continued to talk amidst growing sobs. "I feel like a failure, Mom. A damn big failure who couldn't help the one person who depended on me most."

She was shaking at that point and Rachel continued to pat her soothingly. "It's okay, baby," Rachel repeated, as Sarah's head sank deeper on her shoulder and Rachel slid her arms around her, holding her tight and letting her cry until she could feel the sobs lessen in their intensity.

Finally, wiping her tears, Sarah began to explain everything to her mother. She started from the event she had first witnessed; the driver assaulting Aviela. Then, she told her mother about the young woman she had begun to get to know, and the bond that had developed between them as Aviela began to let down her guard and they worked together to visualize a brighter future for her and her baby. She detailed the various events that occurred from the time she helped Aviela into *Free Soles* until the moment she witnessed Detective Askew and Pastor Portland discussing Aviela's death.

"There was a lot she hadn't told me before she was murdered, Mom. I think that's what got her killed."

Rachel's face suddenly reflected fear for her daughter. Unconsciously, yet firmly, she grabbed Sarah's hand, "What do you think she was hiding?"

"I don't know. There was a lot of mystery about the place she'd been before she went to juvie, and she would never tell me who her baby's daddy was. I never pushed her for details. Now I desperately wish I had," Sarah said as she winced a little from the force of her mother's grip on her hand. Rachel lessened the pressure.

"Who was I to think I could change the world?" Sarah asked, shaking her head and sniffing as she wiped a tear off her face. It was the umpteenth time she was addressing the rhetorical question to herself, and, predictably, she received no reply.

Her mother's voice cut into her thoughts and brought her back to earth, "Now, now, stop belittling yourself. There was nothing you could do. We just have to tell your dad. He can help us figure out what to do."

As if on cue, the front door swung open to reveal Jacob. Beaming, he dropped his briefcase on the floor and extended his arms. "Baby girl!"

Sarah sprung up from the kitchen table and

ran into her dad's embrace, beyond relieved that he was so happy to see her. She could not bear to think of how bad she would have felt if he hadn't been. They were both in tears as he embraced Sarah tightly, resting his head momentarily on hers. "I'm so glad you're home."

Sarah breathed into the feeling of being held safe in his arms, while over her shoulder, Jacob made eye contact with Rachel.

"We need to talk," she mouthed.

CHAPTER TWENTY-ONE

"YOU SURE YOU REMEMBER ALL the instructions?" Agent Luciana asked as she tried to get Jacob to look at her. She could sense the nervousness that pervaded his entire body. Luciana had noted over the years that fear tended to cling like bad perfume to those whom the agent prepped for this kind of job. Luciana knew it took guts for Jacob to do what he was about to do and was not surprised when he looked up and asked, "Why do we have to do this here, in my house?"

Luciana took a deep breath as she closed her notebook. She knew that she had to be careful or she would increase Jacob's anxiety and make him abandon the whole project. Conducting the operation at Jacob's house would make his family more of a target if the pastor and the detective decided that they would "clap back" afterward. "As I said, we want him to talk. Plus, it will be less conspicuous if we place the wire somewhere in your office rather than on your person."

Jacob knew she was right. They had decided against the body wire since Jacob's voice kept fluctuating and he kept talking to his chest during the test run of the operation. He knew the kind of person Askew was; a detective to the core, able to smell danger a mile away. That was part of the reason Jacob had trusted him for so long—the detective always effectively covered his tracks. In addition, he had never known Askew to be someone who ran his mouth when he shouldn't. But now, this was exactly what Jacob *did* need him to do.

"Okay. Now, remember you must get him in the vicinity of your office. But before you actually begin the important part of the conversation, pretend to turn the television on in your office to drown out your conversation. However, after you hit the 'on' button, make sure you hit the 'menu' button to start recording. Then, place the remote on the desk."

It seemed to be a lot for Jacob to take in but he did just fine on the practice run-throughs. "Okay, power, menu, and place remote down," he repeated in a slow whispered tone. "Got it!"

Luciana gave the other agent a look of slight uncertainty. Then, she turned to Rachel, who was watching keenly from the side. "Now for you Rachel, your part is to invite Detective Askew over for dinner. Tell him you want to get together like old times. His arrogant ass will take the bait since he knows it will irritate the hell out of your husband."

A loud thud echoed through the kitchen, causing everyone to jump. The FBI agents quickly composed themselves as they realized the noise had come from Jacob, who, as if in a rehearsed move, had slammed his hand on the table and stormed out of the kitchen. In the living room, still in full view of the kitchen, Jacob removed his tie, flinging it onto a side table as he strode toward the stairs and up to his office, where reverberations from the slammed door rattled windows.

Rachel's voice cut through the confusion clearly visible on the faces of the agents, "I'm sorry Agent Luciana, but you must understand my husband feels helpless."

"No, I understand. We're asking your husband to invite a man who threatened his family into his home. However, he has to understand this is the only way. Without Detective Askew confessing his involvement, we cannot move forward. We only have evidence of him closing Aviela's case without a proper investigation. Yes, we did the DNA test on the sample our guy provided on Pastor Portland, and confirmed what Detective Askew only assumed."

Sarah interrupted, "Wait, but I thought Detective Askew already knew the results."

"No, he was bluffing. The report you saw had

been dummied up by Askew to show the pastor. If Askew had actually run a DNA test, it would have alerted the DNA database and his chain of command would have known he had a solid lead in the case. He didn't want that to happen."

Agent Luciana pulled the test results out of her bag as she heard Jacob yell *fuck* again through his office door, "Detective Askew found out somehow that the pastor was trying to arrange for Aviela to have an abortion. So, the day you saw them in the cemetery, he was calling Pastor Portland's bluff and the pastor took the bait. We're glad you happened to be there to witness the confession. But none of that will do us any good if we don't have it on tape."

Rachel made eye contact with Sarah, who was leaning against the island in the center of the kitchen. "Go check on your father, sweetie."

Just as Sarah began to walk through the kitchen, Jacob barged back into the room, breathing heavily. "Let's get this over with," he said. His eyes seemed a bit bloodshot, and Agent Luciana wondered if he had been drinking to boost his morale.

"You ok, Jacob?" She asked, "Have you been drinking alcohol?"

Jacob paused momentarily before shaking his head in the negative. Without pushing the issue, Agent Luciana pulled out her notebook and continued.

"Rachel, you will welcome him and fix him a

drink, chat with him about old times, ask him how he's been doing, etc. Jacob, you will drive up about fifteen minutes after he arrives. At that point, Rachel, you will act as though you and Askew have been having a wonderful time, reminiscing about the time when you were all in college together, and you can thank him for helping Sarah get the job at the DFCS office. The scene you're setting, Rachel, is that you and Askew are playing a humorous joke on Jacob, but Jacob of course will see it quite differently, and Askew will know that he's likely to be furious."

"So once I'm inside, I have to act like I'm shocked and go straight upstairs to my office?" Jacob asked

"Yes," the agent responded, nodding before continuing, "Rachel can then convey to Askew that she's disturbed to find you so angry, and ask Askew to go talk with you upstairs while she finishes putting dinner on the table."

"What if he leaves?" Jacob asked with a tone of apprehension. He was investing a lot in this plan and he wanted to make sure they were covering all the possible bases.

"He won't! He'll want to talk with you, not to talk you out of being irritated with Rachel, but to continue the conversation you started downtown," Agent Luciana responded cheerfully, while privately thinking *I pray he does not, otherwise this plan fails,* as she watched the family.

CHAPTER TWENTY-TWO

I T WAS ALMOST AS IF there had been another death. Silence reigned as the family and FBI agents stood in the kitchen, stunned. How could they explain the magnitude of the fuckup? That was the question on everyone's minds. As Jacob left the room, gripped by a round of coughing, Agent Carter's eyes fell on Agent Luciana.

Luciana did not look like her radiant self at all. Those who knew her could tell that she was in a mental space where she ought to be avoided. At the office, Luciana had two types of moods, each immediately evident to her coworkers. On days when she was nailing the criminals, she would be extremely warm, jovial and generous. She complimented others, bought drinks for her coworkers after hours, and even occasionally told a joke or two. However, on days when her efforts were unsuccessful, it was better for everyone to avoid her because she could become a bit unpredictable. She'd once threatened to staple a memo to the hand of a colleague who had care-lessly shared an off-color joke; no one was quite sure if this threat itself had been in jest or not.

Luciana was now in the dining room talking agitatedly into her phone. When she was done, she rejoined Jacob, Rachel, Sarah, and Agent Sammie Carter in the kitchen. Jacob had a look of concern as he asked her whom she had been talking to. She scowled before answering that she had been on the phone with her superiors, briefing them on the outcome of the operation.

"Listen up, guys. We're going to have to wrap this up since we couldn't get the evidence we needed." She looked downward wearily and con-tinued, "I tried to get them to agree to an exten-sion but I couldn't."

"But I did hit the 'menu' button. I made sure of that." Jacob argued, looking askance at Agent Luciana.

"I'm sorry Mr. Clarkston. We tested the equipment before and after, so we know it was operable. You simply forgot to hit 'menu,' which would have started the 'record' function," Luci-ana replied as she gestured with her left hand as though in an effort to give credence to her state-ment. She was trying to hide the depth of her disappointment, but she wasn't sure how much longer she could keep up the pretense.

Jacob walked over to the kitchen sink. He felt as if he was about to faint and motioned to

Rachel. "Baby, could you hand me something to drink?"

Rachel opened the refrigerator and gave Jacob a bottled water. She could feel his tension and instinctively tried to mollify him. "Calm down baby."

Then, easing him slowly into a chair she began to massage the back of his neck with her hands; Jacob, however, shrugged his shoulders and quickly rose to his feet. He wanted Rachel to know that he did not want to be comforted—especially in front of these strangers and when it appeared he'd failed at the one thing he'd hoped would allow him to atone for the mistakes he had made. For him, showing that he could protect his family, and particularly his daughter, was vital. He walked toward the agent, "So, what happens now? Is my family going to be safe?"

"We'll leave our agent in front of your house for another week. But that's all the time my boss would allow me to extend our resources to you. We will be keeping tabs on Detective Askew and Pastor Portland. Until we get more evidence, we can't move forward," Luciana said in a resigned tone as she signaled for Agent Carter to help her with the packing up of their surveillance equipment.

While Agent Carter sprang to assist her, Jacob did not seem satisfied with her response. He continued toward the agent until he stood in front of her. "But he threatened to have me killed if I interfered with his money. You do remember that part, when I told him I knew how he got his extra money?"

"Yes, I do. But Jacob, since we don't have anything on tape, there's not much we can do about it," Luciana said as she turned to look at Sarah, who was simply staring out the window.

"That's exactly what he was talking about when he said he didn't need my help anymore and that he had come into a very lucrative extra job." Jacob said tersely, feeling his voice begin to rise. He knew he ought to control himself but he just could not.

Luciana decided to adopt a more formal tone, "Mr. Clarkston, these accusations are serious. We cannot charge anyone based on assumptions. I'm sorry but that angle will not work." Then, as if not quite ready to admit defeat, the agent turned to Sarah.

"Sarah, I know you've said that Aviela never identified the baby's father except to say that it wasn't Gerald. Is there anything else you can remember that might help us in any way?"

In a dispirited tone, Sarah responded, "I've told you everything I know. I even looked through her stuff, searching for some clues but got nothing."

Suddenly, Agent Luciana's face changed. "Wait a minute. You got some of her things?"

"Yes. I picked up her belongings from *Free Soles* the other day. Meia had called me to tell me they had to make space for another child. Sarah began to tear up as she remembered, but Agent Luciana's firm look reminded her to focus on the investigation. "I put her things in a box. I was planning to deliver them to her parents tomorrow."

Agent Luciana felt a tingle of hope, and directed Sarah, more sharply than she intended;

"Go get it!"

Rachel looked at her with such an air of umbrage that Agent Luciana hastened to clarify her intentions, saying apologetically,

"There may be something there that could help us understand the situation better."

Sarah looked at her mom, "It's alright, Mom. She didn't mean any harm," and she excused herself to get the box.

Rachel turned to the agents, "I'm sorry. Things are just a little intense right now."

Luciana responded, "I understand."

Sarah returned carrying a medium-sized box. "I went through her things. She kept a journal, and of course the first thing I thought of was that she might have written about some of the things she wasn't willing to tell me. But she hadn't. She'd written some about the times we spent together, and she said that I was the best thing that had happened to her since she and Gerald broke up, and how much she appreciated Kyle. But there wasn't anything about the father of her baby, or why she was afraid. I looked."

Luciana dropped her bag back in the chair and walked toward Sarah to collect the box.

Agent Luciana could see a small book, covered in sequins, lying on top of what appeared to be neatly folded clothes.

Sarah explained, "I got this for her a couple of months ago. The girls love them because if you push the sequins in one direction, they show one color, and if you push them in the opposite direction," she demonstrated as she spoke, "another color shows."

Aviela's journal had a pink/red heart in the middle of a silver/white background. Sarah thought she couldn't bear to lose this last remnant of the connection they'd shared, and her face showed her ambivalence.

As she handed the book to Luciana, Sarah said hesitantly, "I really would like to keep the journal, if that's ok, since it's all about the new ways she was coming to think about herself, and so much of it was related to the talks we had been having."

Luciana nodded but her eyes were on the book, as she immediately began flipping rapidly through the pages. Suddenly, her body stiffened and her eyes widened. Something had grabbed her attention. She held the journal up triumphantly; "There it is. Jackpot!"

The agent then took a deep breath and looked at Sarah and Rachel and Jacob, who rushed over see what had caused Luciana's excitement.

Peering at the page, they saw the last entry, dated the night Aviela left:

I spoke with Nicole. She is such a nosey house-mate. She said the state would take my baby. I don't believe her. Sarah would not let them do this. Don't know how true it is, but she said she was pregnant by —— I didn't tell her I knew him, because I know she talks too much. I need to find Sarah and tell her what I should have told her in the beginning.

Luciana requested, "Agent Carter, could you come here and get a picture of this?"

"Isn't that the same girl you talked to at *Free Soles* the day Aviela had disappeared?" Rachel asked her daughter, as she took one more look at the blank page.

Before Sarah could respond, Luciana said urgently,

"We need to find this Nicole and speak with her!" her voice regaining its vibrant tone as she saw her case moving forward once again.

Sarah immediately ran to the kitchen table and grabbed her car keys. "Let's go. I know where she is, come with me!"

———

Luciana had known it was vital not to reveal that the FBI was working on the case, and she'd been careful to leave her FBI vest in Sarah's vehicle when they went to *Free Soles*.

Now Nicole followed Agent Luciana out of the study at *Free Soles* where their interview had taken place, and the two went to collect Sarah, who had not been allowed in the room while Luciana interviewed Nicole. Nicole's fearful expression made it clear something serious was afoot, and as the three continued out the front door, Agent Luciana waited momentarily on the porch for Nicole before reaching out to touch her arm reassuringly. She remembered how much time it had taken her to convince Nicole to talk and she knew that the girl was still extremely frightened.

Two hours previously, when Nicole had entered the study and was introduced to the agent, she had immediately turned to Meia and entreated, "Please don't make me say anything about Aviela."

Agent Luciana had been surprised that the girl would make that kind of request, but she'd patiently explained the reason it was important for those who had killed Aviela to be brought to justice—before they could hurt anyone else. Assuring Nicole that Aviela's death was not her fault, she asked her to divulge everything she knew.

When Nicole was ready to talk, Luciana had brought out her recording device and made sure that it was working properly. In between sobs and silences, Nicole described both her own experience and what little she knew of Aviela's.

The hardest part was trying to convince the

girl to testify in court. Nicole's eyes had bulged in terror as she begged not to be forced into any public declaration. She had known of too many people hurt because they'd been caught snitching. It took about 40 more minutes of patiently explaining the concept and specifics of the U.S. Federal Witness Protection Program before Nicole was eventually convinced.

Luciana's face reflected a cacophony of discordant emotions. While anyone could see the agent's excitement, her face also exhibited deep concern. She was reflecting on her talk with Nicole, which had lasted only a few hours in reality but had seemed like an eternity.

The case was at a point where a momentary carelessness on the part of an FBI agent could alert Detective Askew to the investigation. For this reason, the FBI couldn't use the police department; they knew that the detective still had friends there. Such cliques were always tightly knit as one screw-up could open a can of worms for them all.

Luciana summoned Agent Carter and told him that the girl would be placed in protective custody.

CHAPTER TWENTY-THREE

S ARAH PACED BACK AND FORTH as the agents
hooked the wire up to Barbara. She was
simultaneously shocked and worried after hearing that her former supervisor was somehow
connected to Aviela's death. She glanced in the
woman's direction and saw the fear in her eyes.
She'd never seen Barbara in such a condition.
Her sleek brown hair was tied neatly into a bun
and she was formally dressed in pants and a
sharp looking coat, but sweat was trickling down
her face despite the cold winter weather.

Although Sarah had not liked her boss, she'd
had no idea Barbara had been involved in the
criminal enterprise that led to Aviela's death.
Sarah had been stunned when she was told the
FBI had found emails on Barbara's personal laptop discussing at-risk girls who would be good
candidates for the "so-called church youth program." Sarah had looked upon Barbara as a sin-

cere—if burned out—person of principle, despite her grouchiness.

It all came down to this moment. Sarah hoped Barbara would make good on her promise to meet with Detective Askew and get him to confess to trafficking girls. For performing this service for the FBI, Barbara would be given reduced federal prison time.

Once the agents finished testing the wire equipment on Barbara, they reminded her to remain calm and behave as naturally as possible. "That's easy for you to say," Barbara snapped nervously. She was trembling with fear.

"How can I stay calm?"

"Don't worry. We'll be in the area and will move in as soon as he gives the confession," Agent Luciana assured as she handed Barbara a bottle of water. Barbara was beginning to lose her composure.

"Why can't you wait until I leave before you do that? He's going to know I'm the one who gave him away," Barbara demanded urgently, her voice shaking with fear.

Agent Luciana interrupted, "Look, we are running this show. We know you're accustomed to leading, but you lost that privilege a long time ago. Do as we say, and everything will go smoothly. No need to worry about your reputation now."

Barbara gave Luciana a quick cut of the eyes and conceded.

The other agent spoke up, "Now remember; you want to meet with him to discuss new girls you have for the program. Allow him to do all the talking. Try not to go into any particulars. We don't want it to seem like you're leading him." She took a deep breath and rose to her feet. "I just want to get this over with."

The agents gathered their equipment and headed out the back door of FBI headquarters. Luciana grabbed Sarah; "You're riding with me. We'll be in the trail car. I want you to witness your hard work pay off."

Sarah smiled, though she wasn't at all sure whether she was—or should be—more excited or afraid.

"Barbara, make the phone call once you get into your car and onto the highway," Luciana instructed. Barbara nodded.

Barbara got into her county vehicle, a 2015 Chevy Impala. The agents followed in unmarked cars, mostly Ford Mustangs, Jeep Cherokees and Honda Accords. Detective Askew was smart; he couldn't be fooled easily, and he would notice a cop car a mile away.

The agents tailed Barbara at a distance until she got to the meeting spot deep in Wade Walker Park. The agents didn't follow her into the park but positioned their cars in a subdivision directly across from the entrance, sending in a drone to cover Barbara's every move from above.

The location was out of Detective Askew's

jurisdiction. He'd chosen a place where no one would be likely to recognize either of them, and if they did meet someone who knew one of them, he wanted his rendezvous with Barbara to appear to be a social meeting in the park.

Barbara had just pulled her car to the rear of the park when her phone cell rang. She looked around in fright and picked up the phone. She recognized the voice immediately as Detective Askew's.

"Hello" she muttered into the phone. Initially, her vocal cords would not function, but once she cleared her throat she found she could speak almost naturally while her eyes darted furtively in search of the caller.

"Park your car, get out, and walk past the kids' swing set and into the woods," instructed Detective Askew stiffly.

Barbara continued to look around to see if she could spot him, but she saw no one. Her hands began to quiver as she gripped the steering wheel tighter. The chills down her spine spread to her arms. Panicky thoughts raced through her mind. *Was he onto her? Would the wire work in the woods? Was he planning to kill her?* The more she thought, the more terrified she became.

Barbara got out of the car and did as she was told. As she passed by the kids' swing set, she almost screamed with fear as a single swing moved, squeaking in the breeze. Sighing, she wiped the sweat from her forehead and returned her attention to the phone.

"Now what?" she whispered, trying to keep her voice from trembling, "don't you think this will draw attention?" The susurration of leaves behind her caused Barbara to swing around abruptly, dropping the phone. She hastily crouched to pick it up but remained squatting as if hiding from something.

"Where are you?" she inquired anxiously as she scanned the bushes.

Detective Askew's voice instructed, "Now throw the phone into the woods and come out and get into the black SUV parked near the swing set."

Barbara did as she was told; when she came out of the woods there was, indeed, a black SUV parked near the swing set. It had not been there previously and must have shown up when she walked into the woods. When she got close to the vehicle, the driver's side window rolled down, and a man in the passenger seat told her to get in and drive.

Barbara started as she realized she recognized the man. "Wait, aren't you Pastor Portland's driver?"

"Shut up and drive, lady."

As she did, the man took a quick look in the passenger side mirror to make sure they were not being followed. He then returned his attention to Barbara. "Don't try anything stupid. Just drive. No talking."

Barbara drove the black SUV out of the park, following the route the man directed her to take, making a right turn out of the park and onto a narrow two-lane back road that led past several subdivisions.

"Dammit!" A voice shouted over the FBI radio. "Be advised—all units—the subject is pulling into a subdivision. There is no way we can follow now. It would be too obvious."

"All cars back off. I will trail at a distance," Luciana responded, back on the radio. She glanced at Sarah and murmured rhetorically, "What the hell is Askew doing?"

Sarah, feeling totally at sea, simply raised one eyebrow and shook her head to indicate her own bewilderment.

As Barbara drove slowly through the subdivision, she caught a flicker of movement in the rearview mirror and a figure rose up in between the second and third rows of seats. The person's head was covered by a black hood, but although she could not make out the face, Barbara was certain it was Detective Askew.

"Don't look back here, just drive," the figure ordered Barbara, and then "Yo, man pat her down; make sure she clean."

The driver began to run his hands along Barbara's shoulders. As soon as the driver touched Barbara she flinched, and when he got to her breast Barbara slapped his hand away. "Touch me there and I'll break your filthy hands," Barbara flared angrily, her face suddenly hot with color; she was hoping that her indignation would protect her. The man drew back, looking toward the figure in the back of the vehicle.

"It's okay," Detective Askew responded, a taunting note in his voice.

"What the hell is all this sneaky shit Clifford?" Barbara demanded, trying to get just the right tone, but sure that her extreme nervousness was blatantly apparent.

"Just want to make sure you haven't been speaking to no one. My friend here saw FBI agents leaving Pastor Portland's church a week ago and since then he hasn't returned any of my phone calls. Then all of a sudden you call me talking about some new girl. Just trying to make sure we aren't dealing with a rat."

Barbara replied quickly, "I been trying to call him myself to tell him but when he didn't answer, I called you. So, what do you want me to do with the new girls?"

"I want you to get rid of all the files of the girls we sent to Pastor Portland."

"Also, for now, let's lay low!" he said as he cleared his throat, "Send the girls to a foster home until I can find out what's going on."

"Okay, now where're we going?" Barbara asked. She was relieved as she glanced quickly in her sideview mirror and saw a vehicle following them.

"Back to the park for now," Detective Askew responded, as he handed her a new disposable cell phone. "Don't contact me. I will contact you."

Barbara didn't feel as though she had enough information to satisfy the FBI, so she decided to push a little harder.

"What about the money?" she inquired with a bit of a whine. "You told me we would be paid our usual amount, so what's going on with that?"

"Go to the park and you will find your share in the woods near the walking trail. It will be at the half mile mark. Once you're in the woods, walk twenty steps along the path. It will be in a brown paper bag to the left of the path, half-buried under the leaves," instructed Detective Askew.

Barbara pulled the SUV into its former parking spot in the park as Askew dictated. As she turned off the ignition and unbuckled her seatbelt in preparation for getting out however, the vehicle was suddenly swarmed by uniformed FBI agents with their guns drawn. Barbara froze.

Detective Askew squatted in the back seat

and drew his weapon. Looking murderously at Barbara, he screamed, "I'm going to kill this bit..."

But the pastor's driver had inexplicably moved between them, and before Askew could yell at him to get out of the way, the man was flashing a badge as he commanded, "Drop it! Drop the weapon!"

A look of disbelief flashed across Askew's face as he gripped his gun harder.

"FBI! You're under arrest!"

As the two men stared each other down, Barbara whipped open the car door and stumbled clumsily out of the SUV. She ran across the parking lot until she could not run any further, and as she bent over, trying to catch her breath, she felt the warm wetness of urine trickling down her leg.

One of the FBI agents ushered her away from the scene, though she could see, over her shoulder, the agents removing Detective Askew from the vehicle, and the pastor's driver grabbing him and deftly slapping the handcuffs on.

Agent Luciana and Sarah had pulled up just in time to see this, and Sarah was flabbergasted when she saw the pastor's driver with an FBI badge around his neck. *But he killed Aviela....?* She couldn't believe her eyes. "Isn't he one of the guys we were after?" she asked Luciana in bewilderment.

Luciana placed her hand on Sarah's shoulder.

"It was Detective Askew. He wanted the pastor to believe his driver did it, but the driver was actually our agent—he'd already spent a year around the church investigating its leaders for fraud. He'd originally notified our office about his suspicions of sex trafficking, but until recently, there wasn't a lot of hard evidence. But we definitely had our eye on them and when your dad called us with the information you had linking Askew to Pastor Portland, we were pretty sure we could get what we needed to move forth," explained Luciana.

Sarah stared at the pastor's driver, who, after having handed Detective Askew off to another agent, came over to where she and Luciana now stood outside Luciana's car.

Luciana introduced them; "Sarah, this is Agent Rowe." The man extended his hand to shake Sarah's. Without taking it, she snapped, "I saw you assaulting Aviela!"

Agent Rowe looked down steadily into Sarah's eyes and nodded briefly before saying "I knew that's what it must have looked like to you, but no, I was trying to get her to go with me. One of our informants told us she was working for Pastor Portland as a prostitute. I approached her and told her I wanted to speak with her," Agent Rowe explained.

Sarah shook her head slightly, eyes still narrowed with suspicion; "But I saw you push her to the ground."

"No, I whispered in her ear that I could help her and she snatched herself away. I didn't want to cause a scene. When I looked up and saw you staring out the window, I waited to see if you were going to call the police. When you didn't, I made sure to see what car belonged to you so I could get your license plate number in case we needed you later."

Sarah folded her arms, mentally reviewing the various events she'd witnessed and been told of, but she couldn't get them to coalesce into a congruent picture in her mind. There seemed to be too many contradictory incidents and motives. Had she misinterpreted everything?

"What about in the graveyard, when Pastor Portland told Detective Askew that you'd followed Aviela and killed her?" she asked pointedly, after thinking for a while.

"That's what I had told the pastor when I found out she had been murdered. Back when you saw us, he'd wanted me to find her and talk her into getting an abortion. Once she was placed at *Free Soles* I knew she'd be safe, because of all the security measures in place. Of course, when Portland told Askew that I'd murdered the girl, Askew knew it was a lie, but there was no reason for him to correct the pastor.

"After it was on the news that she was dead, Pastor Portland told me he hadn't wanted her dead, he'd just wanted to make sure she didn't have his baby. I didn't say anything. I wanted to see if he would call the police. When he didn't and told me to keep quiet and that he had a detective friend who could make it go away, I played along."

Luciana had been watching this interaction, and at this point she came closer and gave Sarah a comforting side-hug.

"I know, this is a lot to handle. But we couldn't blow Agent Bowe's cover, so we didn't tell you everything."

"But if you didn't kill her, how did you find out Detective Askew had something to do with the murder?" inquired Sarah curiously.

Luciana chimed in, "Well, let's just say our informant knows everyone in the neighborhood. He was in front of your apartment building and saw Detective Askew leaving the woods where Aviela's body was found. One hour later the police were swarming the place."

"Yes, and for once in his life, our informant wasn't too drunk to remember what he saw," chuckled Agent Rowe.

"Informant? Drunk? Building?" Confused, Sarah looked at Luciana. "Wait ... Scooter?"

Luciana smiled, and then turned her head and motioned to the other agents., "Let's wrap things up, team. Good job, but there's still work to do."

Sarah had called Kyle, her parents and Meia as soon as she and Agent Luciana got back into the car on route to the FBI office to let them know about the successful outcome of the sting operation, and Agent Luciana had phoned Aviela's parents, making sure to note the essential nature of Sarah's assistance in getting the information that led them to their daughter's killer.

———

While people were arriving in preparation for the press conference that evening, Luciana went to the coffee machine providentially placed inside the large room and poured herself a round. She could feel her head pounding. She'd slept little the previous two nights, and she could feel the toll it was taking. *Sleep when this is over*, she always reminded herself when she felt the urge to rest.

Totally unexpectedly, Bill and Sandy had gone out of their way to go up to Sarah where she stood talking with Kyle, Jacob and Rachel in the lobby. Bill had even extended his hand to Sarah, saying gruffly, "I know I made a lot of mistakes and I wanted to apologize to you. We had no idea how much you'd done for our daughter, both while she was alive, and after her death to bring her killer to justice... and this whole thing has made me realize that even though you weren't her blood family, you did more for her than we did."

At that moment Bill seemed too emotional to continue, but eventually he did, finally saying, "I shouldn't have kept her from seeing that boy. He wasn't really a bad kid... I just couldn't see it at the time. Anyway, thank you," he finished, and Sandy gave Sarah one of Aviela's latest pictures, a lovely 8 x 10 that showed a smiling Aviela before she'd left home.

Sarah smiled graciously, though she knew that his acknowledgement would take some time for her to absorb, but she simply asked as she collected took the picture,

"Do you mind if I share this when we do the news conference?"

"Not at all. Please do. We want the world to know we are proud of our daughter," Aviela's father said, putting the final icing on the cake as they all filed into the meeting room.

When she saw that people were seated, Agent Luciana began. "Welcome, everyone. This meeting has been called because we will be holding a news conference in about an hour, and we have to prepare what we're going to say." Luciana looked around the room and noticed an unfamiliar face.

She nodded to Kyle and said, "I'm sorry, but who are you?"

As Kyle made to answer, Sarah spoke for him, "This is my dear friend Kyle, who was very fond of Aviela and who supported her, and me, every step of the way."

Agent Luciana nodded, more pleasantly this time, and said, "Then I'm glad you're here."

Kyle smiled and Sarah hitched her chair ever-so-slightly toward his so that they would be close to each other during the briefing.

Agent Luciana now began—slowly and methodically—to read over the list of information they would be releasing to the press.

"First of all, Sarah, we want to thank you. Because of the relationship that you had built with Aviela, she knew that she could turn to you when she was ready. It's tragic that she was killed just as she was preparing to give you the information that would break this sex trafficking ring, but because of your determination to find the identity of her killer, we will be able to bring the perpetrators to justice. It was first-rate detective work, and if you ever want to join the FBI, let us know. I'll put in a good word for you."

Sarah gave Luciana a smile tinged with sadness and responded,

"Well, Aviela gave her life trying to save other lives. I don't want us to lose another person to human trafficking. And thank you, but as much as I appreciate the FBI offer, my work is helping survivors of abuse."

Agent Luciana chuckled, "I understand. But remember the offer is always open.

———————

The walk to the podium was one that Agent Luciana had undertaken many times. Yet, this one felt more personal than the others. As she neared the microphone, she reflected that Aviela had not died in vain.

"Good evening everyone. I'm Agent Luciana Gumez, and I am with the Federal Bureau of Investigations' Atlanta Division. I am here today to announce that arrests have been made of two prominent figures in our community. These figures, who were trusted with the protection of our children, caused them the greatest harm. We wouldn't be here today if it wasn't for two brave women who helped to take down one of Atlanta's largest sex trafficking rings. Ladies and gentlemen, I present Sarah Clarkston and Aviela Scott."

Sarah stepped forward, as it had been agreed that she would, holding up the photo of Aviela for everyone to see. Carefully speaking into the microphone Sarah said, "I want to thank the FBI for all of their hard work on this case, and to tell the public that Aviela's baby boy is currently in the state's custody. We are looking for a family that will be a good fit for him, as well as for families willing to take in the numerous other babies and children who need and deserve loving homes. If you are interested in becoming a foster parent or adopting a child please contact us; your love is urgently needed. Remember, we are *all* God's children. Thank you," and with that she smiled and stepped back from the microphone.

Luciana stepped forward and continued, "As a result of their bravery, we were able to recover multiple girls and one boy from the horrible human trafficking prison in which they were trapped. At this time, we are not able to release much information and will not be taking any questions afterward for the safety and privacy of the survivors.

We can tell you that the operation was being covered up by the church, led by Pastor Richard Portland, and veteran law enforcement officer Detective Clifford Askew. They used the Department of Social Services to target at-risk youth and placed them in a pseudo youth program operated by the church. The minors were housed at a location where johns would come and pay for sex, with the money going to support the pastor's and detective's lavish lifestyles. We will release a list of the charges to the media immediately following this press conference. Thank you very much, ladies and gentlemen. That is all we have currently."

As soon as Luciana left the podium, news reporters started shouting questions. Camera crews jockeyed for position in an effort to get the best footage of Luciana and all those standing on the platform. Moments later, FBI agents escorted Sarah and the panel safely to a back room, where they debriefed.

CHAPTER TWENTY-FOUR

I T HAD BEEN AN EMOTIONAL and difficult period for Jacob and Rachel. following the FBI's investigation. After much deliberation, they had sold their home in Buckhead and bought a more modest one in Columbus, Georgia. For more than twenty-two years they had lived among the elite in Buckhead and were considered great contributors to the wellbeing of the community.

However, after Aviela's death and the revelation of Jacob's prior shady dealings with the now-reviled Detective Askew—he had been spared jail time as a result of his cooperation with the FBI investigation into Aviela's murder—he could not escape the damage to his reputation, or his career, and thus the community's attitude had changed considerably.

Before the incident, whenever Rachel went to the grocery store, she would be greeted cheerfully and with warm pleasantries. However, after all the news coverage, Rachel felt herself the center of unpleasant attention every time she stepped out in public. People seemed uncertain whether they should feel sorry for her, or condemn her as an accomplice in her husband's actions, and the tension was palpable. Jacob, of course, had lost not only his livelihood but also the attendant prestige; he was, however, abundantly grateful not to have lost his wife and daughter as well.

Columbus, the city to which Jacob and Rachel relocated, was perfect for them to bond as a family again. The city was a place where the family could get the peace and quiet they wanted in the rebuilding process. When they moved in, it was as if they were people without any media history. As they went out to the store and other places, no one stopped them awkwardly to ask about the Portland case. Instead, they were greeted warmly and welcome-baskets filled with homemade pies and cakes were left on their wide porch.

Every Saturday, the family participated in the town's tradition of having dinner in downtown Columbus in the square. The live music, great food, and small crowds made them feel young again. When they were there, Rachel would encourage Jacob to participate in the oft-held singing competition. He frequently won, and she would offer to give him his own, personal prize when they returned home.

Recognizing that the crisis, and its attendant move, provided her with a new opportunity to engage in the humanitarian pursuits she'd once loved, Rachel started a nonprofit organization. Recruiting three employees and taking on two interns, she worked vigorously in tandem with Agent Luciana's contacts to create an instructional booklet for the purpose of educating churches, schools and the public on the signs, and dangers, of abuse and human trafficking.

Jacob helped out from time to time, preparing documents and providing informal legal advice where he could. Now barred from the practice of law for 10 years, he had been invited by an old friend, now a professor at the University of Georgia, to be a guest speaker in an ethics class about some of the pressures and pitfalls that might come their way after graduation. It was the kind of talk Jacob might or might not have taken to heart back when he was in school, but he felt better about himself at least offering the information, in the hope that it might prevent even one person from following the incredibly misguided and painful path he had taken.

Even though Sarah had wanted to stay in Atlanta, Luciana had convinced her to follow her parents to Columbus. The DFCS office was undergoing a significant reordering now that Barbara was gone, and although Sarah had been encouraged to contribute suggestions for ways their services could be improved, she agreed that even with the potentially positive changes, the job was probably not an ideal fit for her anymore.

This had spurred her to move, and she chose to live with her parents again. In their newly limited financial circumstances things were easier on all of them if they shared expenses, and Sarah could even afford to go back to school to get her Master's in Social Work.

Rachel supported her daughter's decision to keep learning, but offered daily reminders that God didn't require a degree to qualify those He had already chosen.

When she said this, Sarah would always chuckle and express her appreciation while maintaining that she wanted to be a role model to other young women who had dreams.

Rachel's nonprofit offered Sarah the opportunity to help transform how police departments and social service agencies dealt with abuse survivors. With her experience and education, she became a consultant, educating them on the effects of trauma. Sarah realized that by operating outside the system she had the ability to effect change without being crushed by the exigencies of the daily grind, but she missed many elements of direct service work.

———

One day, when Rachel was washing her hair, the

doorbell rang. "Sarah would you get the door???" Rachel yelled from upstairs.

"Yes, I'll get it," Sarah yelled back as she walked to the door with her laptop in one hand. A tutor was explaining what students could expect on the forthcoming online exam and she paused the program to answer the door.

She opened the door and stepped back, amazed and delighted. "I don't believe this! Meia, what are you doing here?"

Meia laughed, the smile on her face growing even wider. She looked so radiant, though Sarah knew that she was still hard at work taking care of girls who had been rescued. "Well, aren't you going to invite me in to find out?"

With the computer still in her hand, Sarah gave her a warm, one-armed hug. Even though the two women had kept in touch since Sarah left town, she realized that she'd deeply missed seeing Meia in person. She'd been such a source of support during the time after Aviela's death and Sarah hadn't forgotten it. "Come in and have a seat."

Meia followed Sarah to the living room, where they both sat on the sofa.

"It's so good to see you. What's been going on?" Sarah began, as they sat. She closed her laptop, placing it on the adjacent loveseat, and turned to face Meia, who was admiring the interior.

"Well, we've been really busy since the press

conference. A lot of donors have come forward and we were able to purchase one hundred acres of land."

"Oh my God! That's amazing."

Meia smiled and nodded; "Isn't it? but that's not the reason I'm here. I was sent by my board of directors to ask you some questions." Meia heard some footsteps and looked up; Rachel was coming downstairs with a towel wrapped around her head. "Hello, Mrs. Clarkston. You may also want to hear this wonderful news."

Sarah turned around and moved her computer off the loveseat so Rachel could sit down. "Mom! They got donations to build a new facility on a hundred acres of land!"

Meia, still brimming with news, added, "Yes; we're forever grateful for the donation you and Jacob made after selling your Buckhead home. Many of our donors said they were inspired by your kind act."

"It was our pleasure. We wanted to continue the work Aviela started. I mean, I never met her but her bravery and sacrifice has touched our family. We're grateful that Sarah was able to help as much as she did," Rachel said warmly.

"And that's one part of why I'm here," Meia said as she turned to her friend. "Sarah, Aviela was the key to some important information, as you know. Once Aviela knew that she wasn't the only girl Pastor Portland had snared with his spurious religiosity, she was finally able to let go of the misplaced loyalty that had kept her from telling you that he was the father of her baby—as well as Nicole's. And because of the trust you'd built with her, she knew she could ask you for help determining the veracity of Nicole's fears about the babies.

In addition, and hugely important to us going forward, Aviela's struggles emphasized that there are services we need to provide to ensure that pregnant survivors of abuse are sufficiently supported," Meia said.

Just as she was about to continue, Jacob walked through the garage door and placed his bag on the kitchen floor, calling out, "Sarah, Rachel, I'm home. I hope you guys are ready to go get some food cuz I'm starving."

"In here, sweetie." Rachel shouted toward the kitchen.

Jacob walked into the living room, taking off his tie and beginning to unbutton his shirt as he told them, "Whew, the kids were wonderful today. They asked some great questions."

He stopped short when he noticed Meia sitting on the couch, and quickly began rebuttoning his shirt. "I'm sorry—Baby, why didn't you say we had company?"

"Well hello, Mr. Clarkston," Meia said, smiling.

"Dad, they've got land to build a new home for the girls!" Sarah interjected excitedly as she turned back to face Meia.

That's wonderful Meia," Jacob said enthusiastically, but looking at Meia's face, Jacob realized that she had more news to deliver, so he moved over to sit in his recliner and faced her with an inquisitive air.

Meia continued, "As I was saying, we realized Aviela was scared off by the rumor that the state would take the pregnant girls' babies away after they were born because we had no room for them. Even though Nicole's specific concern that her baby would be forcibly removed from her was unwarranted, her observation about the facility's inability to care for infants was correct. It was something we had considered, but we just didn't have the trained staff to deal with babies; or children of any age, for that matter. Nor did we have the funds to cover the costs of insurance and medical care."

"Who knew it was so hard to do the right thing for our children? You would've thought people would be rushing to help," Jacob said. He seemed to remember at just that moment that his own behavior in this area had been far from exemplary, and added, "well, I must admit that I, too, was oblivious to the reality of this problem until Sarah brought it to our attention."

"Brought it to *your* attention," Rachel laughingly reminded him— "it was the reason I've always been so adamant about sending donations to organizations that help survivors of abuse."

Meia smiled and continued, "We wanted

to do more for the girls than just house them. Therefore, we are building a much larger facility, which will fulfill a greater number of our survivors' needs. It will be located on one hundred acres of land with farming, horses, and nature trails, and we'll have a meditation garden named after Aviela."

By now, Sarah was tearing up at the idea of the beauty of such a facility.

"Also, because we recognize the needs of male survivors of abuse, this will enable us to transform the old property into a home for male survivors of abuse and human trafficking."

"I know this is exciting news, and I wanted to share it with you first. However, that's not the only reason I'm here." Meia reached into her leather briefcase and pulled out a manila folder. "Here is the blueprint and a list of some of the programs we will have at the new facility. Sarah, you and Rachel can look them over and tell us what you think."

Sarah reached out, grabbed the folders and passed one to Rachel. After flipping through the glossy photographs and elaborately detailed written description, she enthused,

"This is amazing! I can't wait to visit it once it's up and running!"

"Well, Sarah," Meia said, pausing significantly, "we were hoping that as the new Director of the facility, with your mom as the Assistant Director, you two would give us some ideas on how to make this the only center of its kind in the world."

Sarah let out a small cry of surprise and excitement. "Wow," she said, looking at her mother, "this really is a dream come true, isn't it?"

Rachel nodded, as they all waited for Meia to continue.

"Okay, before I go on, I need an answer from both of you."

"Yes, yes and yes." Rachel and Sarah said in unison, as Jacob grabbed a tissue and blew his nose loudly. "Lord thank you. Lord, thank you for another chance," he said while looking up at the ceiling.

"Well, thank you both. I'm very excited that you're interested in being a part of this venture!" Meia laughed. "I should be getting back to my office," she continued, "but in the back of both folders are the contracts, along with salary and benefit information," Meia informed them as she gathered her belongings and stood up.

"Mom. Grandma would be so proud. Wouldn't she?" Sarah asked as she looked at Rachel.

"Yes, sweetie. She sure would be," Rachel replied as she brushed her daughter's hair back from her face and they all rose to their feet and walked Meia to the front door.

Jacob smiled and commented, "I will finally be able to keep my promise to my mother." After a long and painful road, he had come to realize that true happiness came from having his family happy and safe, and from giving to others so that they could have the same.

"If you don't mind my asking, what promise was that?" Meia asked as she turned around to say goodbye.

"It was a promise based on her favorite biblical scripture, Micah 6:8. She wanted me to use my life to bring justice into the world," Jacob said as he felt more tears forming in his eyes.

"Oh, that's so lovely," Meia said happily. "By the way, Sarah, the board has decided they want you to name the new home. I'll give you a couple of weeks before we file the necessary paperwork with the state to begin the building process."

"No worries. I already have a name," Sarah said almost instantaneously.

"You do?" Jacob and Rachel asked together, surprise written on their faces.

"Yes," Sarah replied as she looked over her shoulder at her dad. She did not need to think too deeply about this. The name had just come to her.

"What will it be, sweetie?" Rachel asked.

"It will be called Micah's Promise."

THE END

ABOUT THE AUTHOR

Kevin McNeil is a retired Special Victims Detective who served twenty years with the DeKalb County, Georgia Police Department. Now an author, motivational speaker and empowerment coach, he has a Bachelor's Degree in Biblical Studies and a Master of Divinity Degree from the Interdenominational Theological Center in Atlanta, Georgia. Through his motivational speaking company, The Twelve Project, Kevin shares his own story of overcoming abuse to motivate others and empower abuse victims to recover their true authentic selves and live out their life's purpose. With over ten years' experience in public speaking and motivating crowds throughout the United States, Kevin is an energetic and powerful speaker who has dedicated his life to raising awareness around abuse issues and fundraising for organizations that promote holistic healing.

Made in the USA
Columbia, SC
03 February 2020